THE NEGATIVE MAN

John Cane, having resigned his commission in the Royal Artillery, is hired for temporary security work. He is asked to investigate a blackmail case involving photographs of a government minister that could be very dangerous. Together with Special Branch's Chief Superintendent Fergus MacDown, Cane pursues his enquiries from a Huntingdonshire burial vault to the Yorkshire Dales. He and MacDown find the blackmailer—but not before they have followed a dangerous and tricky route...

THE NEGATIVE MAN

THE NEGATIVE MAN

by
Philip McCutchan

Dales Large Print Books
Long Preston, North Yorkshire,
England.

British Library Cataloguing in Publication Data.

McCutchan, Philip
   The negative man.

   A catalogue record for this book is
   available from the British Library

   ISBN 1-85389-683-7 pbk

First published in Great Britain by Robert Hale & Company,
1971

Copyright © 1971 by Philip McCutchan

The right of Philip McCutchan to be identified as the
author of this work has been asserted in accordance with
the Copyright, Designs and Patents Act, 1988

Published in Large Print 1997 by arrangement with Philip
McCutchan.

Dales Large Print is an imprint of
Library Magna Books Ltd.
Printed and bound in Great Britain by
T.J. International Ltd., Cornwall, PL28 8RW.

CHAPTER ONE

It was cold, damned cold and wet, and the silence was really getting on my wick. It's all very well to read about churchyards at midnight; you don't realize the half of it until you're physically there, even if it isn't actually midnight, and crouching behind an eighteenth-century tombstone in case the men who are after you start shooting again. You imagine—when that's your current real-life situation—that they'll be creeping round behind you, so you turn, and stare into the darkness, which is so total that in fact you can't see a thing. You can hear an owl hoot somewhere the other side of the church, and you can smell something that could be a fox, but you can't hear or smell anything else unless it's just the overall wet and the rainwater gurgling down into the runaway from the church guttering. You imagine plenty, though, and it isn't necessarily ghosts, and ancient crumbling skeletons beneath rotting, fragmented oak or deal

7

according to station. This was a country churchyard and I was probably above deal; the squire and his relations, as I had already discovered, were round the other side, some of them in a brick vault tacked on to the side of the nave. As a matter of fact, I'd been looking in there; I had seen the coffins through a grille in the side, by the light of my torch, and it had been soon after I'd flicked on that torch that the men had appeared out of the darkness behind me. I'd thought I'd dealt with them but the shooting had started before I had beat it around the East window.

I heard a man's voice: 'Come along, Cane. Better make the best of it. We're going to get you, you know that. Why not make it easy for yourself?'

I kept dead quiet. I didn't know the voice, but I knew now where it was, and fancied its owner hadn't the same handy knowledge about me. If it was dark for me, it was just as dark for him. I took my courage in both hands and did some tombstone-dodging, heading away from the darker loom of the church itself towards the lychgate and the lane that ran past the derelict farm. It was a pity it was derelict, or someone might have heard that earlier shot...but if they had, they would probably have done what the rest of the village down the road seemed to be doing—turn over and go to sleep again, if ever they had woken at all. After all, there are still poachers in the country, and though poachers don't normally use guns, such noisy sporting discharges are not all that remarkable in rural England; not inconceivably, Robert Marton himself could have taken it into his head to emerge from the Hall for a nocturnal rabbit shoot. It all helped to feed the paying guests.

A tree dripped rainwater down my neck, and I jumped and shivered. I made it to yet another tombstone, through the unkept long grass that almost submerged it. Just here, the dead had no caring descendants. My God, it was damp and gloomy and depressing!

Then I heard something.

There had been no audible footsteps on the lane outside, but now I heard the faint click as the latch of the lychgate was lifted and straining my eyes I made out a figure there. My first thought was that the man with the gun had gone on out, but I knew I was wrong when the figure seemed to move in and shut the gate behind him.

He didn't stop for long, not in this world anyway. I reckon the gunman had his wires crossed too. He opened up; I saw the flash and heard the bang, and the dim shadow by the lychgate dropped without a sound.

That gave me my cue, I decided.

I did a tombstone rush after that, keeping low, and reached a hedge that joined the low wall around the lychgate. It was laurel, and I pushed my way through without damage to myself, and arrived on the brink of the deep, muddy pond on the other side. I skirted this in safety and, keeping close to the hedge, went down the lane's grass verge like a bat out of hell. I didn't know who the corpse was, and I reckoned the gunman would still be busily finding out too and saying a few hard words to himself because it wasn't me. At all events, I didn't hear anyone behind me and I reached the Crimonds' cottage in six minutes flat and let myself in. Next morning I got up all bright and fresh for breakfast but Bill Crimond, as usual when on leave, didn't; he was a lazy old bastard really. Eve, his wife, was already having hers when I went down.

'Morning, John,' she said. She grinned

at me. Eve Crimond was dark and gipsy-like, very attractive, and if Bill hadn't been an old friend and former brother officer, well, I guess I'd have been in there like a dose of salts. 'Out on the tiles last night?'

I was about to say yes when I remembered I hadn't taken my car and there weren't many tiles within walking distance of Drayling, not my sort of tiles anyhow. Of course, there was the bus from Henstoke... Anyway, I said, 'No, Eve, darling, no tiles. Just some nice, healthy exercise.'

'In the rain?'

'In the rain,' I said firmly. 'You know, it's bloody lovely, after Aden.'

'Oh, come off it,' she said, pouring coffee and giving me another provoking grin. 'Aden was years ago!'

I said, 'Well, it's not a place you forget quickly, put it that way.'

'Ha, ha,' Eve said. Actually she sounded just a shade worried. Even in the seventies, it probably doesn't help a respectable family to live easily in a village if a guest has taken the baker's daughter behind the barn. So I told her, with absolute genuine honesty, that she could forget all about sin. I said, 'I just wanted a walk all by myself. I said so at the time. And that's all. Truly.'

I wondered what I was going to say when the news broke, but decided I would cross that bridge when I came to it. Of course, it was going to be damned awkward to say the least. Me on a late night prowl, and that body by the lychgate. Or maybe the gun-man would have disposed of it. I hoped like hell he had. As a matter of fact the news, or some of it, broke a damn sight sooner than I'd ever thought it would, since I didn't suppose many of the villagers ever passed through that lychgate except in death, not even on Sundays. They only held a service once a month. The non-resident rector was a very busy cleric: in his spiritual care he had Drayling-cum-Wedderend-cum-Henstoke-cum-Clay End. But I suppose I should have reckoned on the galley wireless. It was Eve's daily woman, Mrs Crawford, who brought the word. She was vibrant with it as she marched in through the door. She didn't even take off her hat and coat and scarf, and she didn't mention the vile weather, before she said, with full dramatic voice, 'He's disappeared, Mrs Crimond. Gone!

Just simply vanished.'

'Who?'

'The squire,' Mrs Crawford answered. The older villagers still thought of him as that. 'Mr Marton himself. There's no trace, no trace at all, and the car's in the garridge. His bed was slept in, that's the funny part. Mrs Marton is beside herself, the poor thing. I don't know, reelly I don't, nobody's safe anywhere these days.'

I didn't say a word; the figure of the night before hadn't got to be Robert Marton anyway, though the coincidence was a trifle pointed. Eve said blankly, 'I don't see why Mrs Marton should be beside herself at all, Mrs Crawford.'

The daily woman bristled. 'Well, I never! Wouldn't you be, if the Major vanished?'

'Yes, if he vanished for long. It's barely nine-thirty. He could have gone out shooting.'

'Could, but hasn't,' Mrs Crawford said briskly. The hat, coat and scarf started to come off now. 'Or that's what I hear, anyway. You mark my words, Mrs Crimond, something nasty has happened, something very nasty. The papers are full of nasty things, that you can't deny. And it's never been like Mr Marton to get up in the middle of the night, and go out, all on his own. He's not the sort.'

She sniffed, and left the room. She was much put out by the reception accorded to her news. Eve had once told me that she and Mrs Crawford had a kind of invisible bond because both their husbands were Scots—exiles, strangers in a friendless Sassenach village. Now the good lady was disappointed with Eve and the tantrum would wreck the morning's work.

'Damn and blast,' Eve said crossly. 'What a fuss about nothing!' Then she looked up at me across the coffee cups. 'You were wandering abroad last night, John. I suppose you didn't knock him off, did you? Or kidnap him?'

'What for?' I asked. 'Now if it had been *Mrs* Marton...'

Eve went off into a peal of laughter. 'I'd doubt that,' she said. 'Didn't you see enough of Phyllis Marton last evening, John?'

'Not last evening,' I said, holding back on the full truth—which was, that earlier I'd seen photographs of her; and of her brother-in-law, more importantly. It was true she was no beauty, but she must have had something. She had; the very

14

revealing photographs had shown it, in detail. I finished my coffee and sprang what I knew would be an immense surprise. I said, 'Eve, I'm humbly sorry, believe me, but I have to get back to London.'

'What?' She couldn't believe it. 'But, John...I don't understand. Isn't this a bit of a *volte-face?*'

I said again, 'I'm sorry. I know it's sudden, dear.'

'Sudden! When do you have to go?'

'Today,' I said.

'Oh, no!' She was genuinely sorry and disappointed. 'You've only just come, and you wanted to see that man Ottershaw... Is this to do with a job?'

'Yes,' I said, and again the intent behind the answer was not entirely honest.

The Crimonds were very old friends. Bill, still in the army, had served with me in the gunners. I had chucked in my commission around four months earlier; I'd got bored with it all, the savour had gone with all the easier conditions of life in the service. You couldn't feel the same pride any more now that kiss me good night sergeant-major tuck me in my little wooden bed was untrue only in so far as the little wooden

15

bed was now a well-sprung mattress and a bedside light. I'm not a snob or a die-hard or a blimp—that was my grandfather's generation—but all the same I do like a touch of smartness and discipline and I do have a certain sense of the fitness of things. I'm not the sort that ever insisted too much on yes sir, no sir and heel clicks; but when the directive comes down the line that the good officer doesn't mind being called Jacko or Bill or Fred by the rank and file, then I reckon it's high time for out. It's even higher time when you feel you can't give an order without it being reported to a man's MP. I felt they would soon be moving the shop stewards in, and that I did not want to see it being run by committee and a show of hands. So I got out with a handshake, but regrettably no pension since I hadn't served for long enough. I had a little money, enough for me not to have to rush into the first job that offered, and I had some experience of what the adverts call man management. I was all set for industry to take advantage of my maturity and judgement and ability to do a thousand and one jobs. Or something. They didn't rush. After a couple of months or so I began to realize I'd been a bloody fool, but by then it was too late and I had to make the best of it. I didn't worry too much; I'm not that sort. But I was feeling the start of the creepy fingers of depression when I met Rudolf Limbrick in Trader Vic's Bar in the London Hilton. It was purely a chance encounter, I was a little tight and I knocked his scotch over and bought him a new one, and we just got talking. And it all led to Drayling, by stages anyway. Because Bill and Eve Crimond happened to live there, I had pricked up my ears when Rudolf Limbrick mentioned the village. Anyway, now I was leaving. I think Eve was sorrier to see me go than Bill; I'd enjoyed talking over old times and regimental gossip with Bill, but I dare say it had bored him stiff, seeing he was still stuck with it and would be back at the depot in another three weeks. Before I left, more news, in a purely negative sense, had come in about Robert Marton, via Mrs Crawford's daughter, who had called in with the twins to enliven mum's morning: no sign had been seen of the squire and he had left no messages with anyone. It seemed he must just have crept out of the house like the cat creeping out of the crypt and that had been that. Why, no one could even guess, unless another woman was involved, but, according to local lore, Robert Marton had never been the man for that kind of carry-on. Stuffy, he was; a good churchgoer when the busy rector could spare the time. A model husband and father, and besides, he had connexions...and didn't I know that! He wouldn't be making things difficult for his brother-in-law.

'Well, would he now?' Mrs Crawford's well-breasted daughter asked, addressing Bill who had just got up. 'I mean to say, *would* 'e?'

'Depends on the temptation,' Bill remarked, with a sidelong glance at Eve. As for me, I felt inclined to suggest they dragged the pond near the lychgate, but of course I didn't. I drove off soon after that, with a good deal on my mind one way and another, and I was pretty glad when the A1 siphoned me past Fiveways Corner and I hadn't far to go to Limbrick's flat. Not too far, that is. Limbrick lived in a luxury block off the Edgeware Road, just along from Marble Arch, and I wanted a word with him rather badly.

When I got there I found he had a visitor, someone I hadn't met before. Limbrick introduced him as Chief Superintendent MacDown of the Special Branch. Certainly from his manner I got the impression he fancied he was someone rather special, but he looked more like an out-of-work cabinet-maker than a top-flight jack.

He gave me a crafty look as we shook hands, and asked me what I'd done with the body. It was meant to be a joke, of course, but I was feeling edgy and I didn't laugh. MacDown said, 'Never mind, laddie, he's been found. Mr Marton has.'

'Where?' I asked, accepting a gin from Limbrick.

'In the pond.'

'Near the lychgate?'

'Aye—a slapdash job, but somebody was in a hurry, and it was handy. Some people never learn.'

'Oh, I don't know,' I said innocently. 'Some people think, and for all I know rightly, that the cops never look in the obvious places—which tends to make them the safest, wouldn't you say?'

'No, I would not,' Chief Superintendent MacDown said. There was a touch of frigidity; once, he would have been an ordinary cop himself. 'And undoubtedly not on this occasion. But I would say you have some special knowledge, Captain Cane. You spoke, am I not right, of the lychgate? I think you had better tell us everything that has happened in Drayling.'

'Okay,' I said. 'That's what I came for, after all.' I know it was silly, but I could almost feel MacDown's skinny arm reaching out and grasping my shoulder.

CHAPTER TWO

That day when I'd first met Rudolf Limbrick in the Hilton and spilt his whisky, I'd seen the vicious temper in his deep-set eyes. It had penetrated, even though I'd been a little tight. A man doesn't like having his drink knocked over, of course, but Limbrick's reaction had gone beyond the normal, I thought. Generally, a man will wait to see if the knocker-over offers an apology and a replacement before looking quite so devilish. Anyway, the look went when I did the right thing, and he became quite friendly; he even bought the next round and we chatted of this and that. I didn't get any impression of being pumped; I suppose I was totally unused to that sort of thing, and to civilian life as a whole. Limbrick, as I was to discover, pumped everybody as a matter of course. It was his life.

We met casually enough from time to time after that, in Trader Vic's, which it seemed we both liked. Once I bumped into him in a pub near the new New Scotland Yard in Victoria Street. Alone. He was always alone. So was I. I was finding London stand-offish and I never seemed to meet anyone I knew. On that occasion he happened to remark that he was off that afternoon into the wilds of the country. Huntingdonshire.

'Really? What part?' I asked.

Limbrick said, 'Place called Drayling.'

'Good God!' I said. 'Small world.'

'How's that?'

'I've heard of the place. I've got some army friends there.' I didn't elaborate, and he nodded without saying anything. He didn't seem interested. But when he'd finished his drink he said, 'I'll only be away a couple of days. Ring me when I get back and we'll have a meal together.' He handed me a card. I ran my fingers over it; it was engraved. This was the first time he'd given me his address.

I said, 'Well, thanks, I will. Enjoy your stay...and come back with some nice, ripe Stilton. It's my favourite cheese.'

He gave a brief smile. 'I'll remember that.' He turned away then and I watched him shouldering his way through the crowd to the door. Limbrick was a powerfully-built man, very thick and heavy and tall, with immense shoulders and a square bald head that looked like a battering ram. A handsome man, in a craggy kind of way. I would have thought women would fall in heaps, but I'd never seen him with one. And I suddenly realized I didn't know a damn thing about him except that he drank pretty often in Trader Vic's Bar, and that his name was Limbrick. Now I knew his address. I also knew the block he lived in was expensive, way beyond my own means.

I gave it four days, so as not to look too eager, then I telephoned. A woman answered, a woman with a low and sultry voice, very sexy. I fancied there was a faint, indeterminate foreign accent that could have been Norwegian. I asked for Mr Limbrick.

'I am sorry, he is not in. Who is this, please?'

'John Cane.'

'Ah, yes, Captain Cane.' The voice brightened into helpfulness. 'I know Rudolf was expecting you to ring. He would like you to come to dinner. I suggest tomorrow. Is this convenient?'

'Yes,' I said. 'Thank you.' I didn't know whether to call her Mrs Limbrick or not. 'Er...what time shall I...?'

'Seven-thirty,' the woman said. 'This is all right?'

'It's fine,' I said.

'Then we shall look forward to seeing you, Captain Cane,' she said, and the line clicked off. That lunch-time, and that night, I avoided Trader Vic's, not wanting to bump into Limbrick before our arranged date. In the afternoon I had an interview for a job. It was something on the sales side of a big textiles outfit, and some of the executives were carrying out interviews and aptitude tests in a private room in a hotel in the Bayswater Road. There were about a dozen candidates, most of them just that much younger than me and some of them positively juvenile and oozing bounce and confidence

23

and aggressive selling ability—horrible, I thought they were. They would sell a sports car to a totally paralysed man and boast about it afterwards. We all had to take part in silly games, and try to sell impossible things to one another, and discuss random-selected subjects in an aggressive manner, and show initiative, and then we each had a private interview with the Sales Manager, a dynamic man in his early thirties with a thrustful chin. He put me right off my stroke by continually slamming his balled right fist into his left palm, a habit to which I'm sure he owed his 'success' in life. I didn't want the job after all this, and I didn't get it. They didn't say so, but I knew what they meant when they smiled politely and said they would be in touch shortly.

I went a little on the booze that night in a pub near my digs. The Elephant, off Kensington Church Street. I didn't feel too bright in the morning, but it wore off during the day and I was okay by the time I rang the bell of Limbrick's expensive flat. Limbrick himself opened the door.

'Nice of you to phone,' he said. 'Come in.'

I went into luxury. I didn't know what

Limbrick's business was, but obviously it paid. The carpeting was wonderful; you sank in at every step. The flat was decorated in green and old gold and it felt really rich. The furniture was exquisite, the antiques were genuine and must have cost a small fortune. It was all beautifully done, including the lighting. The woman who had answered the phone the day before was in the drawing-room, standing in front of a coal fire and holding a martini mixed, by the look of it. She was as sexy as the voice, and damned pretty with it. I envied Limbrick his property, all of it.

He came in behind me and said, 'Cane, this is Vicki Jenssen.' And I guessed I had been right about Scandinavia. Miss Jenssen shook my hand, and it lingered cosily. I wondered if Limbrick had a wife anywhere; he was a man of almost fifty, I'd have said, and I wouldn't have thought he could have kept himself out of marriage all that time.

'Please sit down, Captain Cane,' Vicki Jenssen said. 'What would you like to drink?'

I looked at her own glass and said, 'I rather go for a martini mixed, like you.'

She smiled; it lit her eyes and face.

25

'Good,' she said, and glanced at Limbrick, who fixed the drink. There was something proprietorial about Vicki Jenssen, who must have been rather more than twenty years younger than Limbrick, something that gave me the idea he ate out of her hand. She turned to me again. 'I may call you John, please?'

'Sure,' I said.

'Good. And as you know, I am Vicki. Rudolf has told me much about you, John.'

'Really,' I said inadequately. I felt suddenly out of my depth, wondering just what I had stepped into. I had more than a suspicion it could be crime. That was unfair. Nevertheless, in a sense, I was right. Limbrick didn't give anything away just then, however, though I'd already got the idea he intended making me a proposition. We had two drinks before dinner, with Vicki going in and out of the kitchen from time to time, then we went into the dining room where the table was laid with silver and crystal. It was opulence so, these days, it had to be crime. That was what I thought. Dinner was great: turtle soup, prawns with cream, brandy sauce and rice; *piccate al marsala;* then peaches in red wine. And the Stilton, just right. There was also a superb Gevrey-Chambertin. All this was accompanied by a kind of potted autobiography of Rudolf Limbrick with excerpts, as it were, from Vicki Jenssen, who came from Bergen. And she really was a queen of the frozen north, the Gevrey-Chambertin told me, ash-blonde and lovely, with a wonderfully tanned but basically fair skin. If the tan was fake, it didn't show, and I'd have taken any bet it was a genuine all-over one, nothing missed anywhere. I would have loved a sight of her in a sauna. Briefly, Limbrick had got around. He had been at sea once, as a young man—Merchant Service, and RNR during the war. He'd been on the convoy escorts—Malta, North Atlantic, Russia. After the war he had gone back to the liners, on the Australia run. He had grown tired of the sea and had spent some years in Australia and New Zealand, then South Africa, then America, both North and South. He had been doing, he said with a rocking motion of his hands, this and that.

He'd been doing it profitably, I said.

He said, 'Yes, that's very true.'

His glance met Vicki's and quickly she

said, 'You would like coffee, John?' We had got to that stage, but somehow I felt she had been cued.

'Thank you,' I said, 'I would.'

'I will go and make some,' she said, getting up. She left the room, and Limbrick passed me a leather cigar case. I took a cigar and he lit his and mine. He puffed out a long trail of fragrant smoke—those cigars had probably cost a couple of pounds each—and said quietly, 'You know, Cane, I wasn't just arsing around the world picking up easy money.'

'I didn't think you were,' I said.

He nodded and smiled, then he said, 'I've told you a good deal about myself. Now I'm going to do something that may surprise you until you think about it. I'm going to tell you about *your*self.'

'Oh?'

'Yes. Just very briefly, in summarized form. You're twenty-eight years of age. Educated Perrivale Street Primary, London W 14, made the grade to St Paul's, Hammersmith. Made the grade again from there to Sandhurst, commissioned into the Royal Regiment of Artillery. Served in Hong Kong, Germany and Aden, as well as at home. Good military record

28

except that you tended to buck authority when you thought authority was being hidebound and stupid. Your father, still living, is John Falmer Cane, clerical worker in the Post Office. Your mother, who died two years ago, was Annette Mary, nee Stocker. Her father was a foreman metal worker, employed in Portsmouth Royal Dockyard. Your paternal grandfather was a London bobby, a sergeant of Metropolitan Police. You're unmarried and have never had a really serious girl friend, but you're no woman hater. And currently you're thinking what a bloody idiot you were to chuck up a good career in the army. Also, you're finding your private income doesn't go as far as you thought it would, now you have to pay for your keep in full. That private income comes from investments bought with a legacy from your excellent police-sergeant grandfather, who won a £25,000 premium bond just before he died—and left it mostly to you instead of your father because he was proud of what you'd achieved by getting an army commission. Right?'

Well, I was pretty amazed. I said, 'Yes, right—but how? How did you know all that?'

29

Limbrick said, 'Oh, men talk about themselves, especially when they've had a drink. They reveal more than they imagine, Cane. What they don't tell you can be found out, once you already have the outline.' He lifted his big, hairy-backed hands and rubbed at his eyes. He looked tired, I noticed. 'Tell me honestly—were you fond of your grandfather, the one who left you the money?'

I nodded. 'As a matter of fact, yes. Very.'

'You valued his opinion, Cane?'

Again I nodded. 'Yes.'

'He wouldn't like to think of you drinking around town on his money. You know that?'

I said, 'Yes, I know. He was a bit old-fashioned.'

'And more than a bit worthy. I dare say he had high hopes for you. I know you mean to find a job, but there are better things to do than selling things to people who can't afford them and don't want them. You must know as well as I do that most people in your position drift into selling, into commercial travelling. It's just about the only thing left that you don't need a qualification for.' He paused, then said heavily, 'I repeat, Cane, there are better things. Much better things. Things that can help your country—just as much as serving in the army.'

'Such as?'

'Such as following in your grandfather's footsteps,' Limbrick said.

I laughed in his face. 'Join the police...as a bobby on the beat? Oh, yes, sure! That's bloody likely.'

He shook his head. 'I don't mean that.'

'What do you mean then?'

He said, 'Just listen carefully. When I left the sea, I didn't just drift, whatever my life summary may have sounded like to you. I left with a purpose. I had good contacts, largely men I'd met in the war. I entered Government service. That was what I was travelling on—Government service, as an—well, I can't be too precise at this stage. Let me just say this, Cane.' He bunched his shoulders and frowned across the table at me. 'I'm pretty near the top in my line now. I have wide responsibilities in the field of security. And we can use a man like you. I know you're clean security-wise because I've had a full check put on you in the last few days. You're what we used to call footloose and fancy free—no entanglements, and at present no career. Let me be brutally frank and say, no prospects. But you have that good army record behind you—I happen to know your senior officers were very sorry you left and that they let you go only because they knew an unwilling officer is no good to his regiment or his men, or to morale. Bad point there—but the *only* one. I gather you never in fact *did* let the side down, in spite of your personal feelings. There are two other things. One is this: it's not yes-men we want, with all respect to the army. You fill that requirement. What I would call the Colonel type is no use to us. Do you follow?'

I said, 'Yes. What's the other thing?'

'You told me you had a friend in Drayling. That, as I mentioned, was where I was going when I left London the other day. Your friends, I take it, are a Major and Mrs Crimond?'

'How did you know that?' I asked, amazed again.

Limbrick shrugged. 'A case of putting two and two together, very simple. But this is the point: it so happens that Drayling is germaine to one of our current problems.'

'How?'

'I'll tell you that,' Limbrick said, 'when you've seen some other people and have agreed to be bound by the Official Secrets Act. In the meantime, nothing of what we have been discussing is ever to be mentioned to any living soul. Clear?'

'Clear,' I said. 'Suppose I join—what do I get out of it?'

'A sense of doing a worthwhile job. Plus, for a start, three thousand a year with all expenses paid. Add that to your private income, and you'll live beyond the scale you've become accustomed to in the army. Think well about it, Cane. It's better than flogging refrigerators on a commission basis with an open sack waiting for you when you don't fulfil your quota.' He raised his voice, 'Vicki, where's that coffee?'

A couple of days later Limbrick telephoned me and said he would be in Trader Vic's at 1145 hours. Over a drink he told me to be at an address off the Brompton Road at 1500 hours that afternoon, sharp. I was. It was a sleazy house, very down-at-heel, and the door was opened to me by an old man in shirt-sleeves and with a fag dangling from a corner of his mouth and

33

a trail of nicotine stain running from his upper lip to his nostrils. I was taken to an upstairs room where four men sat stonily behind a long table and for an hour I was closely questioned about every aspect of my life to date and my hopes for the future. Limbrick wasn't there, and I never learned the names of the four men. They were all very top drawer, though, with clipped accents and disapproving eyes and cold manners. When that was over I was sent downstairs where I was taken over by a young man, about my own age, who just chatted to me. After a while he suggested a game of chess. I had never played, which seemed to throw him a little, but he insisted on teaching me. I quite enjoyed it. After that we did the same with mah jong. I didn't quite get the point. Time wore on, however, and in the evening we went down into the basement where there was a tiny bar, with several men and a girl called Judith squashed into it. We drank, and we talked; mostly nonsense, but of course I knew that everything I said was being very carefully noted and would no doubt be sent upstairs for analysis and, for all I knew, computerization. I was told quite casually that I would be spending the night in the house, and the next two nights as well, and I had better ring my landlady without, of course, giving anything away. I was left alone to make the phone call, but I knew it was being listened-in to and my diplomacy, or lack of it, noted as carefully as my earlier conversation. At 2300 hours everyone drifted out of the bar—we had gone back there after a scratch meal in the kitchen—except the girl and me. After a while the girl insisted I go up to her room for a cup of tea—she had a gas ring, she said. I accepted, and once the tea was made she got amorous and wanted me to stay the night. This, of course, was a trap, and I didn't know how to react. She was young and attractive and if I refused they might think I was queer, and everyone knows that queers are not welcomed in security circles because they can be got at. If I acceded, I might still put my foot in it; it probably wasn't done to sleep with colleagues in case you got emotionally involved. So I compromised—rather neatly, I thought.

I said, 'I'd love to, and I'm going to regret this deeply when I retire to my virginal bed, Judith, but somehow I don't fancy the idea of copulation under a microscope—if you get me. You know as well as I do, they've got the bugs and closed-circuit TV on us. Right?'

I'm not sure, but I think she was genuinely disappointed. Anyway, I must have done the right thing. After three days, during which time I underwent a whole lot more test-tube activity, including for absolutely no reason that I could fathom a ride to Kew Gardens and back with one of the men and Judith, I was summoned before the formal board again and had another grilling, at the end of which one of the brass climbed to his feet and reached out a scrawny hand, which I shook.

'Congratulations, Cane,' the man said in a dry voice. 'We shall be delighted to have you join us.'

I said, 'Thank you very much, sir.' After that I went into an adjoining room to be formally entered and to be given a copy of the Official Secrets Act and to sign papers.

I was on the strength. No more worries—anyway, not financial ones—for the time being. I should add that the strength wasn't in fact all that strong. I was only a temporary aide, signed up for a particular job—and what a load of stupid bull to get it!—but it could be made more permanent if I was satisfactory in the performance of my duties. And that phrase had so familiar a ring that I almost felt back in the army again.

'Now I can give you the whole story,' Limbrick said. We were in his flat; Vicki was out shopping. 'It won't take long. You'll have heard of Harold Marton, I expect?'

'No,' I said.

'You don't know the name Marton at all?'

'No.'

'Drayling,' Limbrick said, scratching his shining baldness.

'It still doesn't convey anything.'

'Marton—Robert Marton-lives at the Hall. His family were squires for—oh, some five hundred years I believe. Now, he runs it as a guest house. I'd have thought you'd have known.'

I said, 'I've never *stayed* there. Or even been there. I just know Bill and Eve Crimond, who haven't been there all that long. Have I caught you out in something you didn't know?'

He grinned. 'It doesn't matter. I knew

you'd never *met* any of the Martons, that's the important thing. Anyway, it's not Robert Marton we're concerned about so much as Harold. They're brothers. Harold Marton—the Right Honourable Harold Marton, PC, MP, is a member of the government. A junior minister. To be precise, Minister of State in the Department of Hygiene and Public Sanitation.'

'Ha,' I said, blankly.

'His post isn't all that important, but he's one of the rising younger men, you know, and a personal protégé of the Prime Minister. Big things are expected of him. That is, if he keeps his nose clean. Or rather,' Limbrick added portentously, 'so long as he cannot be seen to have dirtied it, which is much more to the point.'

'*Has* he dirtied it?'

'Yes,' Limbrick said. 'And no minister wants a scandal. More important no *Prime* Minister wants a scandal. And even more important than that, no government with a small majority in the House of Commons can possibly *afford* a scandal. Do you follow?'

'Yes,' I said. 'What has Harold Marton done?'

'This,' Limbrick said, and handed me an envelope. I opened it and peered inside, then shook out a set of photographic prints in colour. I spread them out on the occasional table that stood beside my chair. I wasn't shocked, and I doubt if Limbrick was. What people do in their sex lives is entirely their own affair and I don't suppose more than one in ten of us is completely conventional in bed. Some like one thing, some like another. It's all in the make-up. But Harold Marton's tastes were certainly catholic. I don't think anything had been left out. They say there are thirty-nine positions, but I really wouldn't know; I've never been able to think up more than about a dozen. All those dozen were there. The woman, though she was far from pretty—she was much too horse-faced for me, with a rather mannish cast of face and the beginnings of a moustache which those excellent photographs showed with cruel clarity—was built for sex. The disattraction ceased at the neck. The rest was superb. Breasts, navel, thighs, buttocks, all the lot. I can't go into details but the afforestation was excellent and the constructional details, all of them, all round, were shown in close-up with Harold Marton participating. I had never seen anything like it in my life and the hidden photographer must have really enjoyed his job.

I looked up at Limbrick. 'I take it this is Marton,' I said, 'but surely to goodness it's his own affair?'

'Of course it is—until it becomes public.'

'Oh,' I said.

'There's another thing. You haven't asked who the woman is.'

'No,' I said, 'I haven't, have I? Who is she?'

'His brother's wife,' Limbrick said.

Once again I said, 'Oh.' This time, I'd really got there. I could well imagine the Prime Minister's concern. Such a scandal could bring down the government, and the majority, as Limbrick had indicated, was pitifully small. So were a hell of a lot of the personal majorities in the constituencies. A whole lot of nice fat parliamentary incomes could change hands. I said, 'I assume, of course, that this is a case of blackmail.'

Limbrick nodded. 'Correct. Someone has the negatives. This someone, and we haven't a clue as to who he or she is, means to make use of them—'

'How?' I broke in. 'In what way? These photos can't be used in the Press—'

'No, but they can be made use of *by* the Press, which is a different thing. The Press can always use the *story* those photos tell, and have the actual prints up their sleeve as positive proof. You know as well as I do, plenty of people want to see the government fall. They'll use any weapons that are put into their hands. Some sections of the Press will resort to any dirty trick to score a telling point. We can take it that unless the blackmailer's demands are met, these things'll have a very, very wide distribution. Even to foreign countries—you'll recall, I expect, how often in the past the British public has come to know things in the first instance via the American or Continental papers and magazines?'

'True,' I said. 'Well, what does the blackmailer want?'

'That's the nasty part,' Limbrick said, frowning. 'He's not demanding anything for himself—not directly, that is. He's demanding that the government should not oppose an opposition motion calling for a drastic cut in Corporation Tax.'

'Isn't that a clue in itself?' I asked.

Limbrick made an impatient gesture with his hands. 'Of a sort, but so wide as

41

to be totally useless. We can't investigate every company director from Land's End to John O'Groats! I think you've missed the point, though, Cane.'

'Have I?'

Limbrick said testily, 'God damn it all, man, I don't give a fish's tit for the fate of Corporation Tax, but we can't have government by blackmail, we can't possibly! This raises an extremely dangerous issue, don't you see? It has to be nipped right in the bud, and damn quickly too. It can't be allowed to grow into anything approaching a precedent, or the country'll be in chaos and anarchy!'

He was really moved, really worried and alarmed. I tried to take some of the steam out of the situation. Lightly I said, 'Surely there aren't many opportunities? I mean, I don't suppose all that many ministers or MPs are likely to give blackmailers a chance, do you?'

'Yes,' Limbrick said.

'Oh.' I was a little startled, a little discouraged; maybe I was all green innocence, but I hadn't thought of par-liamentarians in quite such a light, though I don't really know why. They're human. Perhaps it's the pontification on the telly. I said, 'Wait a moment, though. Why doesn't the PM demand Marton's resignation and save everyone a lot of embarrassment? Then there'd be no basis for blackmail.'

'Sounds easy,' Limbrick said, 'but think again. The PM's publicly committed to full approval of Marton and the Press knows it. Any split would scream aloud for a convincing explanation—and believe you me, the opposition Press would dig, dig hard, and dig good! Once found out, the mud would stick tight, resignation or no resignation. In fact it'd look worse if Marton was forced to resign on a phony ticket—the PM covering for the boys. In any case there's still a very useful basis for blackmail, and you can take it from me, we're in business.'

'You know best,' I said. 'So you want me to bowl this thing out and find the man with the negatives?'

'Not all on your own,' Limbrick said. 'We're digging, and have been ever since this thing broke. We haven't got anywhere yet, and–'

'Just a minute. How, exactly, did it break?'

Limbrick tapped the prints. 'These were sent to Downing Street, addressed personally to the Prime Minister. They were opened by the private secretary, who took them direct to the PM. No one else knows—except us, naturally—and the thing was considered too hot to be given to the ordinary police, to the Yard that is. So it came to me. Just for your information, in case you're thinking of asking, the envelope and the writing paper were sent at once for detailed analysis, finger-prints and so on. No help there, none at all. No leads. Frankly, at this moment we're stumped. And the debate on the opposition's Corporation Tax motion takes place in ten days. We haven't much time. If the Government wins, the mud's going to fly and it's curtains for our rulers–'

'Good!' I said unkindly.

'I know you don't mean that, Cane, but I'm going to ask you not even to *think* it, even as a joke, if you can call it a joke. This is the most serious thing for the British public image for a long, long time. Bear that constantly in mind.'

'Right,' I said. 'What, specifically, is to be my part in the negative hunt?'

Limbrick said, 'I want you to go to Drayling. Stay with the Crimonds and get to know the village and the people.

Get to know the Martons, up at the hall. Especially Mrs Marton. Talk to her, get to know who her friends and contacts are. And her enemies. You'll be my eyes and ears on the spot. It's all very handy.' As an afterthought he added, 'You'll be my nose, too.' He laughed; it wasn't much of a witticism, but I gave a dutiful if hollow laugh myself. The thing certainly did stink.

CHAPTER THREE

It was Eve who answered the phone next morning and she sounded pleased to hear my voice. She asked, 'When are you going to come down and see us, John?'

I said, 'This afternoon, if you'll have me. I was wondering if you could put me up for a while.' There was a muttered conversation at the other end and Eve hadn't put her hand very effectively over the mouthpiece, because I heard Bill saying something about this being rather a pierhead jump. Then Eve came back on and said that of course they would both

45

be delighted; Bill was on leave and would be glad of the company. Well, old friends that we were and all that, I had my doubts about anyone wanting a third party around while on leave, but I was under orders to be a bloody nuisance to them so a bloody nuisance I had to be.

I said, 'It's terribly nice of you, Eve. The fact is, I've got the boot from my digs and I thought I might as well take the opportunity of looking around the provinces.'

'What for?'

I said, 'A job, what else?'

'Oh. Well, John, you'll be very welcome to stay as long as you like—'

'Not,' a voice said loudly over Eve's, 'after I've gone back off leave. Sorry, old chap.'

I said, 'Possessive husbands ought to take their wives back off leave with them and live in married quarters. But I'm glad you haven't, Bill. I can do with a spot of country air, after London.'

'See you, then,' Bill said, and rang off. I had a snack lunch, just a sandwich and a glass of bitter in a pub, then collected my car off the street where it had spent its recent life. I made Drayling in two hours flat, driving in past the house that I took to be the Hall. It was big—a central block with wings forming a courtyard—and it was Tudor. It was really beautiful. The courtyard was paved, and there was a fountain in it, and there were well-kept lawns all round. There were several cars in the courtyard and the whole effect was spoiled by the vast notice at the end of the drive which read: DRAYLING HALL GUEST HOUSE. EVERY COMFORT AND CONVEN-IENCE IN OLD WORLD SURROUND-INGS. TERMS MODERATE. UNDER RESIDENT PROPRIETORSHIP. CLUB LICENCE. SHOOTING ARRANGED. A number of past squires would be spinning in the churchyard. Well, of course, times change. A few years ago, a young man wouldn't be living, to some extent, on a Metro bobby's invested wealth.

I lingered for a few minutes thinking thoughts like these, and then drove on to Dove Cottage, Bill's place. It was no Hall but it was nice, and it was peaceful. I liked it much, much better than London. Eve and Bill came out and Bill asked rather sardonically if I was still glad I'd worked my ticket out.

'It's early days to get down-hearted,' I told him.

'Which means you are. Still—never mind. Nice to see you again, John. You'll be able to relax here and get your breath back.'

'That's right,' I said. 'See things in perspective. Down here, you can forget the rat race.'

'I never knew it existed,' Bill said. 'That's one of the nice things about the army—right, Eve darling?' He put his arm around her, possessively. I don't know if it was a subconscious hint; he obviously remembered I'd once had a reputation. She cuddled into him and, God damn it, I was wickedly jealous. Bill opened my boot and yanked my grip out and carried it inside. Eve and I followed. I felt uncomfortable; I was going to have to put on a hell of an act, both in regard to Eve and in regard to not having a job. However, the job-hunting aspect would give me a certain freedom of movement while I was in Drayling.

It was a lovely little cottage, on the small side for a couple with two children, or it would be when the children were bigger—they were four and seven, a girl and a boy—but it appealed to me a lot. Eve took me up the twisty staircase and opened the door of my room. It was tiny but comfortable and it had a view of the north side of the Hall. That could be handy, perhaps.

Eve told me the geography of the cottage, and then fluffed about the bed for a while and said, 'You're worried, John, aren't you? Have you any real ideas about a job?'

I said, 'Not very concrete ones. Except that I want at least two thousand a year with prospects of a hell of a lot more. I'm prepared to work hard, I'm not a clockwatcher, I'm clean, honest, tidy and largely sober. Know of anything, do you?'

She dimpled. 'I'm glad you can still joke, anyway. I know it must be hell for you.'

I said, 'The big problem is, no qualifications. It's a funny thing. You know all the soft soap in the army adverts—how every employer in the land is straining at the leash, ready to snap up ex-officers, because of their wide experience of management and administration and responsibility the moment they're through the barrack gates?'

'Yes.'

'Well, they're not.'

'No, John.'

'Not in London, anyway. I thought perhaps Huntingdon, Cambridge, Stamford, Northampton, even Leicester...what d'you think?'

'It's well worth a try,' she said stoutly.

I thought of something else. 'When does Bill's leave expire?'

'Three weeks. He'll have had a month altogether.'

'And you haven't gone abroad?'

'We can't afford it,' she said frankly. 'We're not working class, we're classed as rich—so we pay through the nose in taxes, don't we? We miss all the hand-outs, never mind if we need them. Bill even brews his own beer now. *And* it's better than the gnat's water you get in a pub. You can try some this evening.'

'Thanks,' I said, and bent to give her a quick brotherly kiss. 'Look, Eve. Seriously, if you happen to have any friends, any contacts...you know what I mean? I'd be very grateful for a word in the right quarter.'

'Well, of course, you don't have to ask. But I don't know who could help round here.'

I coughed, and looked away. 'I passed the big house on the way in—the guest house. D'you know who runs it?'

'Yes,' she said, 'the Martons. The family's had it for generations.'

'Well, I wondered about that. They'd have a lot of useful contacts all around, wouldn't they? Do you know them socially, Eve?'

'Oh, yes,' she said. 'They're very friendly, though I don't know that I like them all that much. Bill loathes them, but we have been to dinner once or twice. Being army, you see, we're All Right.' She laughed.

'So I could be kind of All Right, too?'

She narrowed her eyes. 'Why ever not?' Then she added, 'Do you want to meet them, John?'

I said, 'Yes. You never know, do you?'

'If you want to, I can fix it, I think. But I doubt if the Martons would be much help.'

'Marton,' I said musingly, as if it had just hit me. 'Isn't there a man called Marton in the government?'

'Yes,' she said. 'Robert Marton's brother. He comes down now and again.'

I'll bet he does, I thought. I said, 'Well, there you are. Couldn't be better! Do what you can, my love, won't you?'

She promised she would, and then Bill

yelled up the stairs that it was time for tea, and we went down. After tea Bill and I chatted about the regiment and recalled some of the old times, and at six he got up and went out of the sitting-room and came back with a large jug of his home-brewed beer, which I found excellent and pretty strong. It turned out that it was Eve who actually did the brewing and always had a supply ready for when Bill came home at week-ends and so on. Bill probed me about my career hopes and we talked again about the Martons.

'Queerish bunch,' Bill said, lighting a cigarette and frowning above the smoke. 'Can't stand Marton, myself.'

'Why's that?'

'Oh, I don't know really. Just prejudice, perhaps. I don't like seeing a fine old place like that turned into a tourists' mecca.'

Eve said crossly, 'Don't exaggerate. This isn't the West Country.'

'True. But you know very well what I mean, Eve. We seem to manage better in Scotland. We didn't squander all the family wealth generations ago, so as to leave our descendants to take in the washing.'

'You can't blame the present Martons for that, Bill.'

'I know!' Bill Crimond shifted his body, which was a big one, restlessly. 'Don't always take me so bloody literally, woman! It goes deeper than that. Robert Marton's a greasy customer, and so's his brother, the bloody politician fellow.'

Eve gave a subdued snort and I caught her eye; fractionally, she winked. I remembered Bill's perennial dislike and mistrust of all politicians. I said mildly, 'I'd still like to meet him, Bill. I need to have more than an eye to the main chance now.'

'You're willing to suck up for a job, is that it?'

I winced. 'Put it like that if you want to,' I said. 'I have to earn my bread. I can't bum off you two for ever, now can I?'

'Hrrrmph,' Bill said. There was a silence for a while, then Bill looked at his watch and said, 'All right, then, come on. How about you, Eve?'

'Okay,' she said, getting up.

I asked, 'Where are we gong?'

'Rose and Crown,' Bill said briefly, 'to waste my precious pay on muck that can't hold a candle to my brew.'

'Why, then?'

'Because the chances are, Marton'll be

53

there. He's a fair boozer and he thinks that slumming pays off. It doesn't, the villagers resent it actually, but he seems to believe that losing one's dignity is all part and parcel of the present day and age. You have to be with it, you see. Maybe in some parts of the country, he'd be right. Not here. This is still rural, bigoted, witch-hunting East Anglia. You'll see.'

And we did.

'No,' Bill said, reaching out a hand to haul me back. '*Not* the saloon. The public. Didn't I use the word slumming?'

'Sorry,' I said, and followed him and Eve towards the door of the public bar. It was fairly spit-and-sawdust inside, and fairly crowded too, with farmhands and such. Mostly men, just a couple of girls who looked out of place there. And, of course, Eve, who seemed unusually on edge as though she, too, didn't belong. When we went in there was a hush in the conversation, but this didn't last, and one or two of the men called out good evenings. Bill went to the bar while we sat at a wet deal table, and he came back with two pints and a half of bitter, in plain glasses, not mugs. Personally I loathe mine in a plain glass, and Bill always had until now. We sat and drank and exchanged a few moody words; the place was ghastly. Quite obviously Marton wasn't there. Things went on around us—a few of the old-timers played darts, and others banged away at pin tables. Someone put a coin in a juke-box and our ear-drums began a slow split. Mercifully, when it stopped, no one bothered to start it again. I was beginning to think this couldn't be one of Marton's evenings for slumming when the door opened and Bill Crimond nudged me. 'Here he is,' he said. 'With madam and all!' He drained his glass and pushed it towards me, grinning. Taking the hint I gathered up our three glasses. The moment Marton and his wife showed their faces, silence fell on the Rose and Crown's public bar. It wasn't just a silence, it was a nasty silence, a silence of resentment and dislike. Just one white-haired old gaffer spoke up and said, 'Good evening, Master Robert, and Mrs Robert,' and I guessed he would be some old retainer who remembered the old generation of Martons in the days when the Hall had been the Hall.

Marton was quite brisk and seemingly

unaware of the atmosphere he had created, and of the Crimonds as well. Rubbing his hands together he advanced bouncily on the bar while his wife seated herself at an empty table and crossed her legs. I looked at those legs with a certain hidden knowledge as you might say. Marton called out to the gaffer, 'Evening, Hanley, evening. Hullo there, you chaps.' No answer; Marton passed it off with a cough. 'You'll take a pint, Hanley, won't you? What's it to be?'

'Thank you, Master Robert, but me, well, I reckons as I've 'as all I want. Thank you all the same, sir.'

One of the girls giggled; no one else made a sound. The girl, whose giggle had sounded out like a six-gun salute, went scarlet. Robert Marton said, 'Well, I'm not twisting your arm, Hanley. A large Haig and a gin-and-bitters, Weatherby. Gordon's.'

'Right,' the landlord said. He turned away to his optics. I saw the sweat patches on his shirt beneath the arms. Marton tapped a fifty new penny piece on the bar while he waited; and while he waited I looked back into the body of the room and happened to notice the way Bill Crimond was looking at Mrs Marton. Funny. I don't mean the look, but the fact of his giving it. The look itself was—I'd have sworn—naked sexual desire, and that in spite of what had seemed to be his flippant attitude towards the Martons, her included. Cover for what he felt about her? Eve had said he loathed the Martons. I was pretty sure Eve didn't suspect anything, nor Marton either, and I dare say Bill was always careful and it probably hadn't gone beyond looks. It didn't last for long anyway, it was just a fairly fleeting look really; and when Marton had been served I gave my order, and while the landlord was getting it I heard the sounds, jovial enough ones, that indicated that Marton had spotted Bill and Eve.

'Well, well, if it isn't Crimond. Nice to see you and your good lady, old boy. Don't often come in here, do you?' The voice was over-loud, too boisterously friendly, and I began to see what Bill had meant when he'd said Robert Marton was a greasy customer. 'Brew your own, don't you?'

'That's right.'

'Well, I'm afraid I can't be bothered. I do my saving by coming into the public bar rather than the saloon, don't you know, and of course I like to meet...' His voice tailed away into another cough. 'Meeting' implied some sort of reciprocity and it was much too obvious he wasn't getting any. 'Mind if we come over?'

'A pleasure,' Bill said, glancing in my direction. He got to his feet. As Weatherby drew the three bitters, I watched Marton's wife with considerable interest. I wondered if either of those two was aware she could bring down the government, or at the very least cause considerable embarrassment and a new tarnishing of the British image all over the world. It would be a fair bet Robert Marton didn't know anything about it, but I couldn't be so sure about his wife. Limbrick had stressed that so far as was known brother Harold was in total ignorance of the fact that any photographs had been taken, and nothing had been said to him officially. That might have been considered curious, but Limbrick had explained that total secrecy was considered the best way. The authorities wanted to get the blackmailer, not scare him off. If Harold Marton or his mistress had been questioned, something could have showed. The blackmailer would have got wind of it and would have taken precautions accordingly. And in any case it was most unlikely that questioning Marton would have produced anything useful. He wouldn't be likely to know who the man behind the camera was. That was the official view. All the same, my own private opinion was that something could have leaked through to those participants, that somebody just might have tried to put the squeeze direct on Harold Marton. I believe Limbrick himself felt this could have been the case though he had never actually said so, and that this was one of his reasons for sending me up here to Drayling to sniff around quietly and discreetly.

I joined the party, clutching my contribution.

Bill introduced me. 'Cane?' Marton repeated. 'Cane, Cane, Cane...not one of the Norfolk Canes, by any chance?'

'London and the south,' I said.

'Ah, really. Well. First visit to our part of the country?'

I nodded.

'First impressions good, what?'

'Very good,' I said, catching Eve's eye. 'Bill and Eve are very lucky people.'

'Glad you like the village. Not what it was, of course. Not so *quiet*, don't you know. Motor-bicycles—dreadful! We're rather on the fringe of the industrial Midlands, of course.'

Bill said unkindly, 'Bad for trade, eh, Marton?' He gave Mrs Marton another look, not so dissimilar from that earlier one, and this time I fancied something passed between them, some private giggle. And this time, the woman met the look squarely and just for the briefest instant I saw that whatever it was Bill felt for her, she reciprocated. I say 'whatever she felt', but that's an euphemism really; it was sex, all right. There was a mutual attraction. Well, well, I thought. Nasty! And, for Eve, with dangerous implications. I hoped Bill wouldn't be a bloody fool and get himself involved with Mrs Marton—or, come to that, for Eve's rather dear sake, any other woman. Anyway, the moment passed, and all Marton did was to flush at Bill's last remark about the proximity of the Midlands being bad for trade, and say, 'It's not that. It's ruining the country spirit, the country ways. The people are changing.' I had no doubt that such of 'the people' as were present in the Rose and Crown had heard that. There was still that embarrassing silence, but none of them reacted. Marton turned his attention to Eve, and Bill and Marton's wife began a somewhat cautious—or was that my aroused imagination?—duologue about nothing in particular. Mrs Marton had a peculiarly distinctive voice, patrician in accent, but sexy in tone. She kept on looking at me, just quick but sweeping glances, and I felt I was being summed up hard. I don't know if she saw me as an alternative partner to her brother-in-law, but I couldn't help seeing her as I'd seen her in those photographs of Limbrick's. I imagined the lot. I dare say her sensuality had something to do with her unfortunate face; it was off-putting, and probably few men had ever made passes at her, so she had had to go out for what she wanted. I could have been wrong, it was just an idea. After a while she spoke to me, and gave me the opening I was supposed to be looking for when she asked, in that very clear and distinctive voice, 'What do you do, Mr Cane? Are you in the army too?'

I said I had been. 'I chucked it in,' I told her. 'It became a little constricting.'

She nodded. 'Pointless, perhaps?'

I met her eye. As a matter of fact, she'd hit a nail on the head. 'Yes,' I said. 'It's all very well saying a soldier's

61

job is to prevent war. It may well be, but you grow a little stale when life is one damn exercise after another with the real thing never happening to put you to the test. Except on a small scale like Aden, where you mustn't shoot anyway or the politicians will have your guts for garters. To my mind, a soldier needs war now and again.'

She nodded again; there was a spark of sympathetic understanding in her expression. I expect what she was doing with Harold Marton was a kind of war, an attempt to hit back against the monotony of routine and tax-paying and welcoming the bed-and-breakfast brigade at the Hall, and her husband's obvious dullness. She said, 'So what now?'

I shrugged. 'I don't know. I just don't know.' I caught Bill's eye and he grinned and said to Mrs Marton, 'John could do with a leg up, I fancy. I suppose your husband doesn't know any tycoon who needs a loyal henchman, does he?'

'Ask him,' Phyllis Marton said with a harsh laugh. She butted into her husband's conversation with Eve. 'Robert. Do you know of any tycoon who'd find a job for Mr Cane? Or is it Major Cane?'

'Captain,' I said.

'Captain Cane, then. Do you?'

'You've rather sprung it on me, haven't you?' Marton sounded snappish. 'I'm not exactly in touch with the tycoon world, you know. It's my brother you want, for that.'

Phyllis Marton's voice was expressionless. 'He's the Minister of State at the Department of Hygiene.'

'Really?' I said, sounding reverent. I could feel the atmosphere between husband and wife. It was painfully obvious. Marton said disinterestedly, 'If I hear of anything, I can always get in touch, but I don't hold out any hopes. What's your line, Cane?'

'Gunnery,' I said.

He gave a short, crisp laugh. 'Not much demand, is there!'

'That's what I've found. I'm willing to try anything else.'

'You'll have to, won't you?'

'Yes,' I said, 'and soon. The money's running out.' I was pressing hard, and I think I was embarrassing Bill and Eve—it wasn't in the best of taste, but I wanted to establish a bridgehead as fast as possible and I reckoned I might just be able to do it at the expense of seeming pushing

63

and thick-skinned and brash. I didn't like it, and I realized just how lucky I'd been to meet Limbrick and escape salesmanship—and that thought gave me added impetus, because I had to make a success of this. I said, 'I'd be awfully grateful if you could put me in the way of anything.'

Phyllis Marton said, 'What about old Ottershaw, Robert?'

'Ottershaw, yes.'

'He's always saying he can't get the kind of man he can rely on to manage anything.'

Marton rubbed his jaw. 'True, true. Man's a bore on the subject. Well. I dare say.' He looked at me and sucked in his breath. 'This Ottershaw is staying with us. Another week of him. Something to do with steel, isn't he?' This was to his wife.

'Yes. His works are in Yorkshire.'

Marton said with a laugh, 'You'd probably have to live up there.'

'I don't mind where I live.'

'Well, I could always have a word, I suppose, but no promises, of course.' Marton looked at his watch. 'Heavens, we must get back.' He got to his feet; his wife got up too. 'Nice to see you all. I may be in touch, then, Cane.'

I said, 'Thanks a lot. It's very good of you.'

He nodded and almost pushed his wife out of the bar door ahead of him. Bill gave a laugh and said, 'They've got to get back to turn the bloody beds down for the Ottershaws,' and again I detected an element of cover for true feelings when he bracketed Phyllis Marton with her husband.

After a latish supper I went out on my own, on foot despite a nasty shower, and walked around the village. I wanted to get the feel of the place, and establish my sense of the local geography. Eve, I think, thought I was being tactful and not hanging around them; Bill offered in a half-hearted sort of way to come with me, and suggested we could look in at the Rose and Crown again before we turned in, but I told him not to bother. I knew he had some do-it-yourself decorating to do—the evidence was in the hall in the form of paint pots and dust sheets. There was not a great deal of Drayling. No more than a couple of dozen cottages, all of them except two inhabited by genuine farm workers, the two exceptions having been renovated like the Crimonds' and lived in by, in one case, a retired Wing Commander from RAF Wryton and in the other by an executive from some factory or other in Bedford. There were some new bungalows, with more under construction in the Crimonds' lane, there were two farms, one of them empty and derelict, and there was a council estate on the northern fringe of the village, safely tucked out of sight, though not necessarily of sound, behind a thick belt of trees and a pond. I walked all around, and ended up wet and muddy at the church, which was unlocked as it happened. I went in and looked at the memorials on the walls. They were almost all of Martons, going back for hundreds of years, some of the inscriptions being unreadable. Outside, I found the Marton graves, and the brick-built Marton vault. I bent down to the iron grille that I found protected from the weather by thick ivy about a foot above ground level, and I peered in. Rain dripped down my neck from more ivy above. There was another grille at the other end, and I saw the daylight through, faintly. When my eyes were accustomed to the dark within, I made out the loom of coffins, stacked one on top of the other and some of them standing upright in a row, like a platoon of soldiers, rock-still and silent, all at attention. My gaze came back to the grille itself, for something about it had been bothering me.

I saw what that something was.

The bars of the grille were thickly dusty, but not all over. There were oases of dust-free iron, as though fingers had recently grasped them. Indeed, fingers could have; mine hadn't, but other curious persons, peering in like me, might have laid hold of those bars. Children, possibly. So it wasn't quite that. But it made me look, and when I looked closer I fancied there was fresh cement around the grille's edge, where it had been grouted into the brickwork. Not too obviously fresh—someone, I believed, had made an effort to darken it with earth and mould, which struck me as suspicious in itself—but not by any means old.

It hadn't been there at all long.

Someone had opened that grille fairly recently. Why?

I went back to the graves. I identified Marton's father's and Marton's mother's. Evidently the vault hadn't been in use for some while—Marton's grandparents were in the bare earth as well—so it could be taken as unlikely that any of the current generation of Martons, assuming any had died, would have gone into the vault.

Odd that it should have been opened. Normal maintenance? I doubted it; the graves were not all that well cared for, and grandpa's headstone was well off the vertical.

I bent down again and used my pocket torch, just a pencil flash that I always carry. The light was going now. I shone the beam in. It flickered over the containers of the dead, over cobwebs and big fat spiders. Something rustled, something scuttled. There was any amount of dust around, but some of the coffins were patchy with it, as though a live body had brushed past not so long ago. I was so intent I never heard anything come up behind me and I almost passed out with sheer fright when the voice at my rear end said,

'What's goin on, eh? Who're you?'

I stayed where I was, with my heart pumping away hard and fast. The village bobby, I prayed, let it be the village bobby. But it wasn't. When I had got a grip on myself, and looked round, I saw two men in the fast-fading light.

I got to my feet. I didn't like the look of them; they were dangerous. One, dressed in jeans and a blue anorak, had a pimply face with a scar running from the outer corner of his right eye down to his mouth. The other wore a leather jacket shiny with rain and very tight trousers and had close-cropped hair. Skinhead, I thought. They were both in their very early twenties and were about the hardest faced pair I had ever seen.

'Who are you?' the scarred man asked.

'What's it to do with you?'

They exchanged looks, and the scarred man reached out a hand and seized the lapels of my jacket. 'Listen, mate,' he said. 'We find you arsin' about in a churchyard and shinin' a torch into a vault, right? We get curious. We want to know what you're doin'. So tell us.' He jerked my jacket right up, nearly throttling me. Much more of this, and I would half kill him, but Limbrick wouldn't like that. It wouldn't be discretion.

I said in a muffled voice, 'Like you, I was curious. That's all.'

'Bloody likely.'

'Likely or not, it's the truth. There's a

69

fascination about vaults and coffins. Are you going to let go of me?'

'What if I don't?'

'I've been in the army,' I said. 'I've done some commando training. If you don't let go, I'll do a permanent injury that your girl friends won't appreciate at all. They'll crack like bantam's eggs.'

There was a silence; the man's grip relaxed a little. He was playing safe up to a point, but he wasn't letting go altogether. 'You one of the Martons?' he asked.

'No. Should I be?'

'It's their bloody vault, innit, and you talk like one of the toffee-nosed lot. All right, so if you're not a Marton, who are you?'

I thought fast. I saw no real point in not giving this man my name; it wouldn't be likely to convey a thing to him or his mate. I didn't know what they were after, but it was a fair assumption it would be nothing more important than, say, lead from the church roof. They didn't impinge on my job. I said, 'My name's John Cane, Captain Cane.'

'Where from?'

'London...but staying in the village with friends.'

'What friends?'

I said, 'Never you mind.' I didn't want to involve Bill and Eve in anything nasty, and I had the idea they just might get a reaction if these yobs were from the local council estate.

'Tell us.'

'Get stuffed,' I snapped.

My jacket was hoisted again. Risks were being taken now, so it had to be important to these two. It was pretty dark now and there wouldn't be anyone around to hear any beatings up. I used all my low-life commando knowledge and I brought my knee up hard and fast and accurate and at the dead right angle. I doubt if anything actually cracked but I knew it would be a long, long time before that scarred man went womanizing again, if only because he would be embarrassed by the heavy bruising and the goose-egg expansion. And he didn't like it. His grip came off at once and he gave a scream of agony and held himself tight. I gave his mate a back-hander across the face that almost made him swallow the loosened teeth, then I drove my right fist smack into his gut and he doubled like the scarred man.

Then I beat it, but not for long. I

had to take cover behind the first of the tombstones when the shooting started. It was dark now but not yet too dark for my moving figure to be picked up, and the man with the gun had been fairly accurate with his first shot. I don't know who was firing, but for injury reasons doubted if it could be either of the two men I'd met, so assumed a third had come up from somewhere. I kept dead still behind my tombstone, dead still and quiet, hardly even breathing. When the darkness thickened in the total way it does in wooded country I shifted tombstones, and made it around the East window, and then gradually did my heading-for-the-lychgate act, and then Robert Marton chose his unfortunate moment to appear.

'And that's it,' I said to Limbrick and Chief Superintendent MacDown. 'I haven't any idea who they were, but I thought it best to get to hell out of Drayling this morning and come back and report as soon as possible.'

'Why did you think that, Captain Cane?' MacDown enquired. He was a dried-up sort of man, with a peaky face and a disconcerting way of directing his spiky grey eyebrows, like antennae, at me, and he sounded tired and irritable and fed-up, as though he'd heard everything before and nothing new was left. 'You didn't feel, shall we say, that you had left unfinished work behind you?'

'No, I didn't,' I said sharply. 'As I saw it, my usefulness in Drayling was over. I did a lot of thinking during the night. Those men knew who I was—though not what my job was—and I could have begun to stand out a mile. Maybe I was wrong to say who I was.' I added. 'Also, Marton was dead.'

'You examined him?'

'No, but I've seen men shot before. Plenty of them. The whole feeling was of death. And he *was*. We know that.'

'Ha,' MacDown said. He sounded sardonic; I didn't like him. 'True, we know it *now.*'

I said, 'Well, if I was wrong to come back, I was wrong. If either of you can explain *why* I was wrong, I suppose it's not too late to go back again.'

Limbrick shook his head. 'No, Cane. You did the right thing.'

MacDown looked astonished. '*Did* he, sir?'

'Yes. We'll switch the line of enquiry. MacDown...didn't Captain Cane's description of those men ring any bells in your head?'

Cautiously MacDown said, 'Aye, they did. Not that I see the connexion, but they sound uncommonly like a pair I recall from my days in C Department at the Yard.'

'Care to give them names, Chief Superintendent?'

'Aye, I will. Lemmon and Clapp. Pair of tearaways. It took me a while, I remember, to get them, but get them I did. Just kids, too.'

'And their crime?' Limbrick caught my eye.

MacDown said, 'Robbing churches, cathedrals mostly. Chalices and the like—articles of great value.' He rubbed at his eyes, wearily, worldly-wise and worn. 'I'd doubt if there's much of great value lying around in Drayling parish church, Mr Limbrick.'

Limbrick nodded. 'That's true in a sense, I'm sure. This is no coincidence, though. I'd better explain. I've had some information. Lemmon and Clapp and another man—'

'Wait,' MacDown said, holding up a

74

hand. 'One moment, now. Phillips. He was the other who worked with them, always.'

'He still does,' Limbrick said. He got up and went across that opulent drawing-room of his and came back with a decanter of scotch and some glasses on a tray. 'And all three of them have recently been in contact with—a man called Ottershaw.'

I saw the way he was looking at me. I said, 'There's a man called Ottershaw staying with the Martons. A steel man, from Yorkshire. Or did I tell you that?'

'No, you didn't, but I knew it anyway. That's why we're shifting the line of enquiry, and that, possibly to your own surprise, Cane, is why I say you did right to leave the vicinity.' He poured three large whiskies. 'You have some more travelling to do, Cane. And you'll do well to remember you're up against some very nasty people. I think,' he added, as he held his glass up to the sunlight streaming through the window, and squinted through it critically, 'there's something the Chief Superintendent hasn't told us about Mr Lemmon.'

'Aye, there is,' MacDown said. 'Rape and murder. A young lassie...just seventeen. The same age as my own daughter.

We couldn't pin it on him, but we know he did it. *We know.*' I saw the way his grip tightened on the glass in his hand, and I wasn't surprised when it suddenly shattered. Whisky flowed; blood mingled with it. MacDown, looking startled, said, 'I'm sorry, Mr Limbrick.'

'It's all right, MacDown.'

'I'd like to get Lemmon, sir, I would like to get him very much indeed.'

Limbrick said, 'We're going to.' He looked at me again. I asked, 'Which was Lemmon, Chief Superintendent?'

'The one with the scar.'

I nodded. I was glad, very glad, of what I'd done to Mr Lemmon the night before.

CHAPTER FOUR

No time was wasted after that. I was ordered north to sniff around the Ottershaw patch, and I went up the M1, fast, with Chief Superintendent MacDown. We went in a vast black Humber, with MacDown driving. Limbrick had said there was just a chance my car had been spotted in Drayling and its number noted. He didn't want any unnecessary risks taken. Before we left he elaborated on what he had heard. He admitted there might be nothing in it, and that if there was, then Lemmon, Clapp and Phillips were way off their normal beat; and he agreed with MacDown that mostly criminals tended to be specialists like anybody else these days.

'But I still don't like the link with Ottershaw,' he said. 'My information, by the way, is retrospective. Two months ago, those men went up to Yorkshire, to a place called Beelby in the West Riding. It's not far from Leeds. They were known to call at Ottershaw's steelworks, which is in Beelby. A few days after that, they called at his home near Boroughbridge—Carnforth House. Now Ottershaw turns up in Drayling—staying with the Martons. Not quite where one would normally expect to find a man like Ottershaw. Ottershaw can afford the best hotels. With all respect to the dead, Marton was an amateur, and amateurs don't usually make the best caterers.'

'Maybe Ottershaw liked the peace and quiet,' MacDown said.

'Maybe Ottershaw wanted to buy the place and set himself as a country squire,' I said.

'Maybe both,' Limbrick agreed, 'but I doubt the likelihood of either! I feel there's a closer connexion. Remember Ottershaw's an industrialist and his company presumably pays Corporation Tax— and there's something else as well: Ottershaw is a bitter man, so I'm told, a man who detests all government interference and all taxation. I suppose we all do—but Ottershaw has quite a bee in his bonnet about it. That's precisely the kind of man we're looking for.'

'A nutter?' MacDown suggested.

'Yes, I think he has to be. And,' he added, 'don't forget our fresh knowledge: that Lemmon, Clapp and Phillips were up to something in Drayling. It all comes together.'

MacDown said, 'Aye, but what does it add up to? Can you tell me that?

'No, I can't,' Limbrick said with a grin. 'That's what you're going to find out. Make for the Bull Hotel in Boroughbridge. I'll fix rooms for you while you're in transit. And remember, this stays in the family.'

'What,' I asked MacDown after we had hit the M1, 'did he mean by the reference to the family.'

'Oh, that,' MacDown said. 'Just that we're not to take the local police into our confidence, that's all.'

'In other words, we don't get any help?'

'Aye, that's right.'

I sat back and relaxed and watched the motorway stream past us like a broad river. I quite liked being driven for a change; it almost made me feel I was back in the army, with a soldier driver. We stopped once, for a cup of coffee and some petrol, at the Leicester Forest East service station. Then we pressed on, leaving the M1 for the M18 and then the good old Great North Road for Boroughbridge, which looked nice and old-world with its grey stone houses. We checked in at the Bull, then went along to the bar for a drink. Over a pint of bitter MacDown told me, quietly, that he was going out for a look-see.

'What about me?'

'You stay here. It's better that way.'

I didn't quite see why, but I didn't argue; the bar was comfortable and the beer was good. There was a very attractive girl behind the bar. I asked, 'Going to Carnforth House?'

Macdown nodded. 'Only to spy out the ground, that's all. I'll not be setting foot on Ottershaw's land. Not yet. I'll not be long.'

I said, 'I'll wait for you, then. Before I go in for dinner, I mean.'

'Just as you wish, Mr Cane,' he said indifferently—he'd dropped the 'Captain' on leaving London, maybe to emphasize my new status—and swigged down his beer, and left the bar. His shoes, I noticed, were badly down-at-heel; he was a tatty little man and he didn't really go with the Humber. Nevertheless, there was something about Chief Superintendent MacDown that gave a man confidence; and, now that he had gone and left me, for however short a time, I felt naked. This was, after all, my first job. Drayling hadn't been quite the same; there, I'd been with Bill and Eve Crimond and had been to some extent wrapped again in the good old army blanket so I'd felt nice and safe and warm. Now I was on my own, in a totally strange part of the country—I'd never served at Catterick or any of the northern army stations—and I had no friends handy and, in the absence of the real professional, I was in a sense In Charge. If anything should happen, I would probably go and make a cock of it. Not that anything was likely to happen in the bar of the Bull Hotel.

I went and got myself another pint. I tried to chat up the girl behind the bar, but not with any success. She was polite, but distant.

MacDown was a long time.

I began to worry when he had been gone two hours and after another half hour I felt it was up to me to do something about it, but I hadn't the faintest idea what. It was difficult, since MacDown had the car. Carnforth House was eight miles away, a very long walk indeed. It was much too late to hope to fix up any self-drive hire, even if the facilities existed at all in Boroughbridge. But when MacDown had been gone three hours I knew I couldn't let the matter rest, so I asked the girl in the bar if I could have a word with the manager. She went away to find out, then came back and led me to his office. I explained about my friend; he'd gone out on a piece of business that shouldn't have taken him long and I was dead worried. Was there *any* hope of getting hold of a self-drive hire car?

'I wouldn't think so,' the manager said, shaking his head. He seemed a decent sort, and helpful; but no one likes lending their car to strangers, which was what I was angling for even though I'd known already I was on a loser. 'Very sorry, Mr Cane, but I don't know of any cars for hire. Reeds'll be shut now. Why not ring for a taxi? There's a man in the town. I'll fix it for you.'

His hand was on the telephone, but I stopped him. MacDown wouldn't thank me for bringing a taxi driver into the affair, nor would Limbrick. 'Never mind,' I said. 'I'll manage. He may be back soon.'

I left the office and, because I had a nasty premonition that something had happened, I left the hotel as well and started walking towards Carnforth House, turning left off the A1 a little to the north of the small town and heading in the general direction of Ripon. I walked as fast as I could, hoping to see the Humber bearing down on me. I didn't. It was ten-thirty by the time I came into the vicinity of Carnforth House, after asking the way in a village; and of course it was dark. But I had a stroke of luck after that and in spite of the darkness I found the Humber drawn off the road into some trees some way short of Ottershaw's residence. There was no sign of MacDown, and the car was locked. I was sure now that something nasty had happened but I had no idea what to do next, other than storm up to Carnforth House and demand to know what they had done with my friend. For obvious reasons, that would scarcely be on.

I was looking around more or less hopelessly when I heard the sound. It was a voice, coming from the darkness, from the trees to my right. It was a monotonous sound of cursing—foul, bitter and Scottish, low but vibrant with pain and fury.

I followed it, using my torch, and found Chief Superintendent MacDown. He was lying on the ground, his face white. He said, 'Man, man, ye've been a hell of a time coming.'

'I had to walk,' I pointed out. 'I was damn lucky to find you at all. What happened?'

'Bloody mantrap,' MacDown said. 'Can you not see that?'

I moved the torch. MacDown's right calf was held fast, nipped almost through by immensely strong iron teeth. There was a lot of blood. I drew in my breath sharply. 'My God,' I said. 'Aren't they illegal?'

'A thought that doesn't free me from the bloody thing, Mr Cane,' MacDown snapped. 'Get you down on the ground, for heaven's sake, and open the jaws.'

I did as he said. It was a fight, but I won. The spring was real power and I could hold the jaws open only just long enough for MacDown to move his leg out and then, when I let go, they snapped shut again with a jerk that sent them flying from my hands to jangle at the end of the securing chain, the end of which was anchored in a concrete block embedded in the earth.

I helped MacDown to his feet, or rather to his good foot. He hopped, and cursed. He was in extreme pain. He said, 'You'll have to drive, of course. Take me to a hospital. I'll need an anti-tetanus jab.'

'You'll need more than that,' I said as we moved slowly for the car. 'You'll need to be in bed for a while.'

'To hell with bloody bed,' MacDown said through his clenched teeth.

I decided he could argue that with the doctor in casualty. 'How did you get into that thing?' I asked.

'Why, I put my bloody foot down and the bloody thing—'

'I know the mechanics, Mr MacDown,' I said. 'But I thought you didn't mean to go on Ottershaw's land?'

'I changed my mind,' MacDown said savagely. 'There's no law against it that I'm aware of.' He didn't seem to want to elaborate, so I kept my mouth shut—and, when we reached a hospital, they kept MacDown in spite of his vehement protests. He had lost a lot of blood, they said. There would probably be some infection, and he couldn't possibly walk on it. Definitely. Nor could they just encase it in plaster for support. With such a wound, that would be asking for trouble. The doctor let slip the word gangrene and MacDown caved in.

'Have your own way, then,' he snapped, 'but you'll not keep me in here long.'

I said good-bye to Macdown and asked when visiting hours were. MacDown glared. 'No such thing as visiting hours,' he said. 'I'm having a private room or none at all. In the meantime, Mr Cane, you'll have to take over. You're as wise as I am, anyway.'

I left him to it and drove back to Boroughbridge in the Humber. I had a good night's sleep and in the morning, after breakfast, I told the manager my friend had had an accident and was currently in hospital but otherwise all was well. Not knowing what I should do next, I decided I might as well find out if Ottershaw had returned home yet from Drayling, for what that might be worth. I think I had some vague idea in my head that if he was still down south, comparatively speaking, a breaking-and-entering job could yield information, always provided he hadn't left any staff in residence, of course. Quite probably he had. The best way of finding out would be a telephone call, so I found a public call box and rang Ottershaw's number.

It was answered, and I said I represented The Employers' National Rock Assurance, or some such, and was Mr Ottershaw at home?

I had a shock. 'No,' said Mrs Phyllis Marton's unmistakable voice, 'Mr Ottershaw is at the works in Beelby.'

'Thank you,' I managed to say. 'Maybe

I'll ring him there.' I rang off; evidently Ottershaw *had* come back from Drayling, anyway—but why with Phyllis Marton? Kindly act towards a new widow? Or was there something else behind it?

I shoved open the door of the call box and stepped out into the sunlight shining down on Boroughbridge. Then I had my second shock of the morning. A man with a pimply and badly scarred face was standing there, blocking my path and grinning at me. Lemmon, the child rapist and murderer according to MacDown.

'I had a funny little feelin' we was goin' to meet again,' Lemmon jerked a thumb towards a seedy-looking Zodiac parked by the kerb, and in it I saw Clapp, the leather-jacketed skinhead. Clapp looked happy to see me and I wasn't surprised. I was the evidence against him and Lemmon, or maybe it had been Phillips, on the charge of murdering Robert Marton, and I dare say they'd been hunting me pretty diligently ever since. Lemmon said, 'Get in.'

'Not bloody likely.'

Lemmon produced a flick-knife. I could just see the slim blade, poking from his fist. He would know how to use it, all right.

He said, 'I don't believe you're going to try your muckin' army tricks here in broad daylight, *Mister* Cane, but if you do, the moment you show movement I go into action first, all right?'

'What applies to me,' I said, 'applies to you too.'

'Huh?'

'I mean, the broad daylight's shining on you as well, isn't it? You're not going to try anything either, and you know it. How's your love life been the last day or so?'

'What's that got to do with anything?'

I smiled, icily. 'Just this: you're due for the same again if you move that knife a fraction of an inch. You know already, I'm fast. And while you're lying on the pavement, Mr Lemmon, all handy for the police to pick up, your pal in the Zodiac leaves you to it and beats it for his own safety. And you know that too. So stop putting on such a damn stupid bluff.'

Lemmon's face was a picture of sheer furious frustration; he knew how right I was, and knew too that he'd under-estimated me. He still held the knife in his fist, but he started backing away towards the car. He hissed, 'All right, so you win for now. Just for now. You're goin' to wish you'd never bin bloody born, you are. That's fair warnin'.'

'Very fair,' I agreed. He backed right up to the car and got in, and his pal drove him away, fast, heading left for York. I made a mental note of the car's number, but didn't expect it to help much. The Zodiac was probably stolen anyway, and would be ditched before long. I was rather glad MacDown hadn't been there. His training would probably have held, but on the other hand it might not; he'd been upset yesterday, when talking of Lemmon. He'd taken that child murder to some extent personally, and he might have found himself unable to resist taking Lemmon in on a charge of possessing an offensive weapon. Limbrick wouldn't want that. Lemmon and Clapp, and Phillips, had to be more frugally used: they had to be free to lead us to the truth.

And I felt they were going to.

I went again to see MacDown, in hospital in Ripon. I felt I should report developments to him. He didn't seem too bad, and was able to take an interest. A gleam came into his eye when I told him about those tearaways, and he said I had done the right thing in letting them get clear. 'They'll be back,' he said with a good deal of unkind satisfaction. 'You're the magnet, Mr Cane. You'll be exercising a strong pull or my name's not Fergus MacDown. But I wish we could see the wood for the trees.'

'How d'you mean?' I asked. We could talk without reservation, for MacDown had got his way about a private room.

MacDown tapped me on the arm. 'I have to keep reminding myself I'm no longer in C Department. It's hard. I mustn't just see Lemmon as a villain who has to be got on a murder charge. I have another job to do now. What I'm saying is this, Mr Cane: I wish to God we could find the connexion between those three and the photographs that form the subject of our enquiry.

'If there is one,' I said.

'Aye, if there is one. Mr Limbrick seemed to believe there was. He's a man that's seldom wrong. Meanwhile, you'll be aware of the date, of course.'

I said, 'Sure. Not long to go before that opposition motion comes up. I'm wondering if I ought to go to Carnforth House.'

He pursed his lips. 'You're quite sure the voice was Mrs Marton's?' I'd told him the reason why I'd been in the call box.

I said, 'Yes, positive. It's a distinctive voice, once heard, never forgotten.'

'They often sound different on the telephone. It's quite surprising.'

'I'm still sure.'

'Aha. Then—yes—I suggest you talk to her, Mr Cane. But not at Carnforth House. You must arrange to bump into her accidentally. You'll see the wisdom in that.'

'Yes, I suppose I do. But I don't see *how* I bump into her accidentally. It could happen over a period of time, but we don't have too much of that, do we?'

'No,' MacDown said complacently, 'we do not! You must use your initiative, Mr Cane, I'm sure you must have plenty. As for me, I'm confined to my bed of sickness till the bloody doctors say I can get up from it.' He looked disconsolate and managed to give a convincingly agonized grimace as he moved his bad leg, but I think really he had decided to enjoy his inactivity after all. There was a very wicked look in his eye as he, in effect, handed the whole lot over to me. I left him to it and drove

91

back to Boroughbridge, wondering how I could fix a chance meeting with Phyllis Marton. Maybe, I thought, if I hung around the Ottershaw works in Beelby, down by Leeds, she might turn up there sometime with Ottershaw himself—but I dropped that one. It would take far too long, and anyway she might be lying low. The newspapers, of course, had got the story now—not about the photographs or the blackmail, but about Marton's murder, and for a day or two she would be front-page news. As a matter of fact Macdown had been reading all the papers when I'd gone in to see him, but he hadn't commented and I didn't find anything of interest in the reports myself. But that evening, after I'd wasted a day in indecision and worry, I bought a local evening paper and there was the solution. Ottershaw was a big man locally, and now he was part of national news, however temporarily. Thus, that local rag made quite a lot out of the fact that he had been generous enough to bring the murdered man's widow up to Yorkshire to stay with him for a few days. Well, her whereabouts were now common knowledge. And I, of course, just happened to be in Boroughbridge! Job-hunting, which

Phyllis Marton already knew.

What more natural—to a brash, insensitive career seeker—than to call with condolences and, as ever, with that eye to the main chance? After all, I'd met the woman the very evening of the tragedy...

Better, however, to let another night's water go under the bridge and call at Carnforth House in the morning, when, with luck, Ottershaw should be in Beelby.

It was only after I'd come to this decision that I asked myself what the devil I was going to say to her. I knew what I had to find out, but I was damned if I could see any good lead-in to a discussion on nude photography and advanced sexual techniques in technicolour. However, always an optimist, or nearly always, I reflected, as I sat in the bar of the Bull, that something would come to me.

It did, though not in quite the way I had intended.

Next morning was crisp and fine, with a fresh wind blowing white puffs of cloud across a blue sky. At least, it started that way, but by the time I had the car on the road a long line of black cloud was rising behind Thirsk and creeping up to blot out the fine day with rain. That rain hit me before I reached Carnforth House, and it came down in sheets that were almost too much for the windscreen wipers and I felt as though I were driving through a river. I almost missed the entry to Ottershaw's drive and the only reason I didn't was that somebody was positioned to make sure I stopped. A figure jumped out into the road in front of me, and I stepped hard on the footbrake and wrenched the wheel round to the right. I just missed the bloody fool who had jumped. He approached my window with a hat pulled low over his eyes and I wound the window down savagely to start slanging him, but I didn't get a chance when Lemmon's fist, wearing a knuckle-duster, slammed into my face. Streaming blood I fell sideways, and Lemmon, reaching in, got the door open and came in with a gun. Stretching across me he flipped off the lock on the near-side rear door and shoved it open, and Clapp loomed up, also with a gun, and got in as well.

Lemmon said, 'Just act sensibly, mate. Move out from under the wheel. You don't have a muckin' chance.'

I hadn't and I knew it. I moved into

the front passenger seat and brought out my handkerchief. All my teeth felt loose, though I hadn't actually lost any, and my lip was split. The handkerchief went red. Lemmon frisked me then got the car moving and headed along the road for Ripon. Feeling stupid I asked, 'Where are you taking me?'

'You'll see.' he gave a hard laugh. 'In case you're feelin' full of wonder, we thought you'd show up sooner or later seein' as how the Marton woman's whereabouts was in the paper. Well, we didn't have to wait too long, eh Bugs?'

Bugs was evidently Clapp, who said from the back, where he was holding his gun pointing at me steadily, 'Long enough, silly bleeder. Needs a good 'ammerin', shovin' 'is muckin' nose in at all!'

'Sure,' Lemmon agreed. 'Maybe he's goin' to get a hammerin', Bugs. In fact, he is.'

'Can't wait,' Clapp said.

I asked, 'What's the point of hammering me?'

'So you talk.'

'What about?'

'Ah, don't give me that!'

'But I—'

'Shut up. You'll talk soon.'

'That's all very well, but–'

'You 'eard what the man said.' Clapp's gun-muzzle screwed into the back of my neck, hard. I shut up. I was only wasting my breath. I watched the road, noting the route. They didn't seem to mind that—I'd have thought they'd have put me right out, so I wouldn't know where I was going, and the fact they were not bothering was significant, I thought, and sinister. We went right through Ripon and picked up a road that I saw was the A6108 signposted for Masham and Leyburn. Lemmon drove dangerously fast, and I noticed that he was watching the petrol gauge, which wasn't too healthy. We did the twenty odd miles to Leyburn in excellent time and stopped for petrol at a garage on the junction with the A684 from Northallerton. I was given a relevant warning before we pulled in, and I kept my mouth shut to prevent a massacre. Clapp and Lemmon had their guns well hidden but still very close at hand, and I didn't want to involve any innocent bystanders.

Topped right up, we went on and headed for Wensley and West Witton. Lemmon said, 'Give your eyes a last treat, mate. We're headin' through the Dales.'

'What do you mean by last?'

Lemmon laughed. 'You'll see. Like the country, do you?'

I said, 'Yes. Don't tell me *you* do.'

He glanced sideways. 'Why shouldn't I?'

'I'd have thought a street corner was more your line, somehow.'

'Maybe it is, for now. Till I've made me mark. One day, I'll pack it in, won't I? Retire, like anybody else. But earlier than most. I wouldn't mind buyin' a place up here. There's room to expand here.'

I wasn't in the mood for sight-seeing, but I did look out at it all, and what I saw, I liked. The day was blue and fine and windy again, and the white clouds were flying over the Pennine peaks, casting fleeting shadows on the green sweep of the Dales beneath. It was magnificent country, wide open, majestic, unspoilt to all the horizons, and a bubbling river ran over rocks alongside the road. We went fast through Wensleydale and left Aysgarth behind and then, just before Bainbridge, Lemmon pulled the car rather suddenly right, following a signpost for Stalling Busk and Semerwater. We were now on a track rather than a road; the contrast was remarkable. At once, we appeared to leave civilization behind; we hurried back into the past. Even Lemmon was forced to drive slowly now; there was only just room for the car between the dry-stone walls, and the surface was terrible. We were descending a pretty steep hillside, and we had left all traffic, all habitation, in another world. Our own car sounds apart, there was a total and brooding silence. It was unnerving, for I sensed that journey's end for me lay somewhere down in the depths of the dale ahead, down by Stalling Busk, which was probably just a collection of half a dozen or so farm cottages. However, we didn't go to Stalling Busk. Ahead just where we began climbing again, the road divided, forming a T-junction. Stalling Busk lay left, and Lemmon turned right, and once again we started a descent. As we came down I saw a biggish lake, ringed with flat mud, with trees beyond it, and the distant high peaks of the Pennines closing us in. That would be Semerwater, no doubt.

It looked like the back of beyond—lovely, but remote. And lonely—terribly lonely. Anything could happen here, and as likely as not it would be a matter of weeks before any human soul came past to see. And a body might never be found.

I shivered.

Lemmon looked sideways and grinned at me knowingly. 'Scared, eh?'

I said, 'Just interested.'

There was a scornful laugh from behind me and Clapp said, 'Interested, my arse. Somebody just walked over 'is grave.' He gave a nasty little snigger. 'Or drove over it!'

Lemmon said, 'Then he's way out. His grave'll be a watery one, very. That is, of course, unless he talks.'

Clapp expressed agreement. 'Think 'e will, do you?'

Lemmon said, 'Oh, sure. He'd better anyway.'

I might not have existed. Unconsulted, I was driven on, down and down into the dale. We approached the level of Semerwater, and I smelt dankness and more loneliness. Just before we reached the lake Lemmon pulled off the rutted track and we lurched across country, following some other tyre marks leading around a thick belt of trees. On the other side of the trees was a solitary cottage, ramshackle and with its windows boarded up and its roof in holes. It had probably been a shepherd's cottage, once, long ago. Now its use was to be very different. I think I had a tomb in mind.

The car stopped and Lemmon told me to get out.

I did so. I got out into cold, invigorating air. Clapp came out behind me. I wanted to go for them both, but I have a respect for guns, and around here shots would be even more unremarkable than they had been in Drayling churchyard. A natural hazard of country life which a townsman wouldn't always appreciate.

'Keep ahead of us,' Lemmon ordered. 'Walk to the door and give it a shove, and after that, be careful.'

I went ahead, along an overgrown path leading from a low stone wall to the cottage door. I gave the wood a hard shove, and the door almost collapsed inwards, hanging from one rusted hinge. I went in, heeding Lemmon's warning. I stumbled over debris and nearly took my head off on a beam hanging down from the roof above. Savagely, I swore. The beam had some nasty nails, rotten with rust, sticking out of it. The place smelt dank and fusty and filthy, as though it had been used as a make-shift lavatory over many years. There was, of course, no light other than what came through the broken-down front doorway.

Lemmon said, 'Right, stop where you are.'

'I'm stopped already,' I snapped. Lemmon came up behind me and ran his hands over me, then told me to turn round. I did. He went through my pockets with meticulous care, even examining the contents of my wallet and feeling my jacket lining all over—a much more thorough search than the frisking I'd had when they got in the car. Lemmon didn't say what he was looking for; when he had finished he said angrily, 'Sit down. Go on, get down on the floor.'

I did so. It was almost bare earth; the boards had largely rotted away long since. It was damp and foetid and my hands contacted slugs, fat black ones, the sort that have eyes on the ends of horns.

'Now what?' I asked.

I saw the daylight shining on the metal of the guns, and then I saw the flick-knife in Lemmon's other hand. I could see his face as well, and I didn't like it. It was as though the man hoped I wouldn't talk too readily, just so that he could relieve some of his sadistic feelings. I thought once again about the girl he was said to have murdered and I pondered the wisdom of two things: the way the Judges' Rules so often inhibited a police prosecution, and the abolition of the death penalty.

Lemmon answered my question. He said, as he brought the knife-blade down close to my face, 'Let's have it all, Cane. The lot. What you were doin' in that churchyard, and what makes you so interested in the muckin' Marton family.'

I said, 'You won't believe this, but there's nothing to tell you. I've told already. I was just morbidly curious. Lots of people are, you know.'

'Sure. And you're right, I don't believe it. What about Marton's wife? What's your interest there?'

I shrugged. 'I met her in Drayling, that's all. I thought it might be a nice gesture to call and say I was sorry about her husband's death.'

'No need to wrap it up,' Lemmon said. 'When you mean murder, say it, we don't mind. Why should we? But that's interestin' in itself, and it's somethin' you're goin' to talk about.'

'I don't follow.'

'Don't you?' The knife came closer; so did Lemmon's pimply face. 'Listen. The newspapers've got the murder report, sure. But there's been nothing about the circumstances—you know what I mean. Nobody by the name of Mister Cane told the police about a ruckus with two blokes by the vault, or about gunfire. Now, that's funny. Very funny. But it doesn't make me laugh. No. You know what?'

'What?' I asked, all innocence.

Lemmon said, 'It makes me muckin' wonder, mate, just where you fit in. You're workin' for someone and me, I want to know who that someone is. Right?'

'Wrong,' I said. 'You're quite wrong. I'm not working for anyone at all. I'm just job-hunting, that's all. I can't tell you anything else, I'm sorry.'

'Not so sorry as you're going to be,' Lemmon said, and his hand moved downward.

CHAPTER FIVE

I knew they were going to kill me; I knew that, because they had nothing to lose by doing so and they could have a lot to gain. I was still the one and only witness to Robert Marton's murder. But they meant to take their time over it and when Lemmon's hand had come down in that vicious motion it hadn't been the hand with the knife. It had been the hand with the gun, and the barrel hit me a nasty blow on the head that knocked me sideways so that I sprawled in the dust and debris and looked up into both gun-muzzles and a pair of happily leering faces full of confidence.

'That's just a start,' Lemmon promised.

I set my teeth and waited. I tried to fix my mind on something else, but I couldn't find any very pleasant images: just Chief Superintendent MacDown taking his ease in his hospital bed, and Limbrick drinking scotch in Trader Vic's in the London Hilton. I began to realize how a rat must feel when it has been driven into a corner. The beating-up was efficient, well-practised, and thorough, and it was interspersed with questions, but I never said a word all through. I hoped Limbrick would appreciate it.

I was quite surprised when, after all, they didn't kill me. In the end I passed out, and when I came round again I heard them talking. They were angry, all right; but, evidently as a result of orders from above, not to the point of murder. I heard Clapp, the skinhead, say: 'He'll be okay down there. Who's ever goin' to look, eh? We won't be gone all that long, either.'

'I s'pose it's all we can do,' Lemmon said, by way of grudging agreement.

''Course it is.'

'Never thought for a moment the bastard wouldn't talk, Bugs.' Lemmon sounded dead worried; somebody, somewhere, wasn't going to like him over this. If I could discover who the somebody was, this whole thing would no doubt become a good deal clearer. I supposed it could be Ottershaw, but there was still nothing to go on. I lay still and kept quiet, hoping to hear some more, but I was out of luck because

Lemmon bent down beside me and shone a torch in my face. I blinked. Lemmon said to Clapp, 'He's comin' round now. Give us a hand and we'll get him down right away.'

Clapp said, 'The drop'll finish 'im off, won't it?'

There was a laugh. 'See if I muckin' care, mate.'

'Maybe *you* won't.'

I waited, on tenterhooks, to hear who would; but again no luck. Lemmon blew out his breath and said, 'Oh, all right, sod it. There's a rope out in the shed. Get it.'

Clapp went out.

I felt Lemmon's boot in my guts and I opened my eyes, blearily. 'On yer feet,' Lemmon said roughly. He still held the gun, and the knife. I did as he said, staggering back against the wall. I could barely see for the puffiness around my eyes, and I felt bruised all over. I felt sick, too, and I had a pounding headache.

'Listen,' Lemmon said. 'one more chance, then we're goin', but you're stayin' till we come back. After that, well, I don't know. Depends.'

'What on?' I asked.

'Never you mind. Now—you goin' to talk, or do you go down the muckin' well?'

'I'm not talking about anything,' I answered, 'so I suppose I go down the muckin' well.'

'You won't laugh,' Lemmon promised.

I didn't suppose I would. Clapp came back in, carrying several fathoms of decayed-looking rope, thinnish stuff. Lemmon took this and tested it for strength. 'Seems okay,' he said. 'Cover 'im, Bugs.'

Clapp shoved his gun in my guts. Lemmon said, 'Move back to the wall and turn around. Put your hands behind your back. Quick now!'

I shrugged and did as he'd said. I heard some cutting going on behind me, and felt Clapp's gun nudging into my spine. Then Lemmon looped some of the rope around my wrists, and hauled it taut and secured it. It felt like a well-done job. After that he tied my ankles with equal efficiency. Lastly I was swivelled round by Clapp on a word from Lemmon, and Lemmon used a dirty handkerchief, backed up with another piece of rope, to gag me; and after that the main part of the rope was threaded over my tied wrists and I was picked up and carried outside. They took me round to the back of the derelict cottage and down what had once been a garden to a well. I was dumped on the ground beside it while Clapp removed the wooden cover. There was no bucket and no rope and the winding handle was missing and the cover was only just about holding together. I was lifted up and set on the lip of the brickwork with the rope rove between my wrists, and Lemmon and Clapp pulled it through until it was two level lengths. Then they both came up close and, holding fast to the rope, levered me off the edge with their free hands.

I wooshed downward at speed until Lemmon and Clapp got full control of the rope, and then my way checked. After that I was let down fairly slowly and I was able to take a good look at my prison. The walls, which were in a pretty poor condition, were slimy and foul and covered with horrible life—slugs and that. At the bottom was an inky-black pool, currently reflecting a small segment of sky through the open top of the well, and the images of Clapp's and Lemmon's heads peering down behind me. The whole place stank; it was more like a drain than a well, nothing pure about it at all. I dropped the last feet, because one of my lowerers had made a balls of his job and let his end of the rope slip. I dropped into that horrid inky pool and for a moment fancied I was going to drown in filth. I went right under; then I hit bottom painfully, which indicated that the level of water wasn't all that high, and I managed to sit up and splutter mucky water out from behind the gag; and found that even while sitting my head was nicely clear of the water.

There was a lot of snarling going on up top, echoing down to me, and I saw the faces looking, and heard Lemmon say, 'He's all right, no fuss. Pull the rope up now, Bugs.'

I felt the movement, the slither of the free end of rope coming up past my wrists. It sailed away towards freedom, dripping water down on me. As soon as it was clear of the top, the wooden cover was banged into place.

After that it was dark. Dark, still, silent. Just like the grave. There were small cracks in the wood of the cover that stood out with the daylight, but that wasn't enough to penetrate to my depth. It was a deep, deep well. I couldn't see a thing.

It was cold too. Desperately cold. After a while I couldn't stop the shivers that racked my body.

It really did feel like the end now. I could never survive this. Lemmon had overplayed his hand and when the boss came he would find a corpse. Lemmon would catch it but that wouldn't help me. I sat in that water in a complete daze, wondering why in hell I'd ever been such a bloody fool as to get mixed up in this. When I had rejected the whole idea of salesmanship as a career, it had never occurred to me that the alternative was to freeze to smelly death in a well in the Yorkshire Dales. And it wasn't just the terrible, bone-penetrating cold of that icy still water: it was the whole concept of where I was, and the stink that filled my mouth and nostrils and lungs with every foul breath. The emanations of years, decades perhaps, of dank water and droppings from above—God alone knew what had been chucked down from time to time if chance visitors had removed that wooden cover—and the dead bodies of slugs and rats and whatever. The water had a nasty slimy scum on its surface, thick and foul. It would probably be green in colour, I thought, if I could see it.

The daylight faded from the cover's cracks. Night was falling. After a while, as I sat in that dreadful numb daze, I heard a drumming on the cover. It echoed weirdly throughout the cavernous well: rain. Heavy rain. Torrential! A new worry came to me: *would the water-level rise?* I wasn't too sure of the mechanics of wells—and I was damn sure Lemmon wasn't either—but it seemed a fair assumption that once heavy rain soaked into the earth, wells rose. That was their function.

It was just a question of time. Time, and the density of the soil, I supposed. Maybe they would come for me in time. In this new anxiety I even managed to forget the cold for a while. Tied as I was, I certainly couldn't keep my head above water by swimming, and even floating would be difficult with my hands fast behind my back.

I think I must have slept for a while, because the next thing I remember was seeing daylight again behind the cover's cracks, but only a thin daylight, and the drumming of the rain seemed if anything to have increased.

It went on for hours. Once again, daylight faded.

During that night, the water level did increase. Sitting, it rose to my chin; my ears were under when I held my head back. I scrambled with difficulty to my roped feet as the water-pressure began to lighten me, to lift me and sway me. I was in a very poor way indeed by this time, and in trying to right myself I fell, crashing down helplessly into the rising, stinking water. I heard my own scream in my ears, filling the well. I hit my head on the brick sides, and felt a blackness come down, but I managed to fight it off, and I floundered about, teetering on my bound feet, trying to hop with the weight-taking assistance of the water itself, though God knows there was precious little buoyancy in it. Later, even standing, so precariously, the level rose to my waist and I knew I dare not sit again.

Once more sheer weakness and weariness made me lurch and I felt very close to death as I fell again into the filth and the rising scum; and then, as something sharp bit hard into the calf of my leg, I screamed again, and bobbed about, trying with a terrible desperation to escape whatever it was that was attacking me. I think that at one moment I was on the very brink of going clean out of my mind. Once more I found myself, as I thought, attacked; but this time a mere pinprick. And nothing followed me, I realized; there was no quick, flashing movement through the water, no squirm of water-snake or subterranean, primeval fish. The object was stationary.

I steadied. I steadied and thought.

I moved back through the water towards that object, although I still felt dreadfully and eerily afraid. Unreasonably so. With my thighs I felt for its shape, its outline; and after a while I was sure.

Someone, sometime, had dropped a scythe blade down.

God, but it gave me fresh strength when I was free of those ropes! I felt fit for anything; it was almost incredible to me. The psychological lift was immense. And it hadn't been too difficult. The blade had come to rest against the brickwork with its point uppermost, and the remnant of its shaft had bedded down in the mud below, so to some extent it was held steady. Very, very carefully I had placed my wrists beneath the blade, against the cutting edge, and drawn the ropes slowly but tightly across it. It was still sharp enough to do the job, and once my hands were free I got the gag and the ankle ropes off with no trouble at all.

As I say, the effect was practically electric. Even the air, which I could now suck in unimpeded by Lemmon's filthy handkerchief, seemed sweeter.

I was going to get out.

I swelled with determination.

The brick sides were surely climbable! On my way down, in the full daylight through the open lid, I had seen the state of those bricks—they were old and crumbly, and the pointing had largely gone. There would be footholds. Trembling with eagerness now, I removed my shoes and socks, bare feet would be more nimble, more sensitive.

I started climbing at once; I felt no need now for rest, and I hadn't the patience. My one overwhelming desire was to get out, out into the good fresh air, the clean air, and away. Away past Semerwater to the main road running through the Dales, where I would get a lift from a passing car to the nearest telephone, the nearest bath, the nearest food and drink.

I found I had been right and the brickwork provided good footholds and finger-holds. I made progress, staring upwards intently, fixing all my desire on the cover, through which, once again, a thin dawn was seeping. The drumming had stopped; the rain had gone now. It would soon be bright day, out there. Bright day.

I climbed. Slowly and carefully, slipping now and again but making net progress. The light behind the lid grew stronger, and nearer. Inch by inch. I was conscious of no effort, only of a determination to attain my objective.

It all went very nicely until my reaching fingers found the part where the construction narrowed, where the wall began to slope inwards towards the top. I don't for the life of me know why I hadn't thought of that; I suppose my mind was too full of excitement and maybe I wasn't registering as well as I'd thought I was, after all those interminable hours of filth and horror and despair, suddenly released in blind hope. Anyway, I was I suppose within a foot or two of success, of freedom, when I realized I wasn't going to make it, that no man could hold on by toes and fingertips when suspended backwards over the long drop, in a far worse predicament than an old-time sailor trying to make it over the futtock-shrouds into the maintop. And down here, there wasn't the unseamanlike alternative of the lubber's hole.

All the same, I persisted. I persisted until, literally, I dropped. I dropped clear from the rise of the narrowing side, smack into the scummy filth below. Just then, I was thankful it had risen. Even so, I just touched bottom before rising up through it, sick at heart and in the stomach too.

There was no hope now. I didn't try again. But it was still nice to have my hands and feet free. For one thing, I was well able to keep my head above water now. For another I could grasp that scythe blade. Grasp it and wait for Lemmon to come down. He would have to do that, or someone would if they wanted to get me out of here in due course. A bound man couldn't be expected to hang on to a lowered rope, after all.

It was to be a long wait yet, but they did come back for me. The next day, I believe it was, though I was in such a state now that I had no real idea of time or even of how many daylights had passed over the lid of the well.

I didn't hear anything until that lid came off. The sudden hard light that came down blinded me temporarily. I slid my body under the surface of the water for concealment. Then I heard a man's voice, Lemmon's, calling to me.

'You all right, Cane?'

I didn't answer and he called again, more urgently this time. Weakly I called back, 'I'm still here if that's what you mean. Get me out, for God's sake get me out.'

I heard a sound of relief, a whistling breath. They still wanted me alive, though I didn't see why. There was a short conversation up top and then Lemmon called, 'Okay, we're going' to get you up. I'm comin' down.'

Fine, I thought, thank God it's going to be Lemmon. That bastard was due for a very big surprise. I was going to kill him; once again my mind was fixed, and it was fixed firmly and to the exclusion of all other considerations upon Lemmon's death. My one side reflexion was that MacDown would be delighted. If the law couldn't get Lemmon, I could. I wasn't directly below the open top and the light didn't reach me, so I was able to move around the perimeter of the surface and grab the scythe. I got it in my hands and ran a finger along its edge: sharp enough! And the point was lovely. It would sink in deep. I intended to take him in the chest, or, if he presented a different target, to cut his head from his body with a sweep right through the neck. I could hardly wait. I was trembling with a terrible anticipation.

After some delay, a rope snaked down and its end hit the water with a tiny splash. There was another brief delay and I saw two faces peering down, Lemmon's and that of another man I hadn't seen before. No Clapp, which probably explained why Lemmon was making the descent. If Clapp had been there, he would have been given the dirty work. It was going to be interesting to find out who the newcomer was. The boss, maybe, the big man?

Lemmon hoisted himself on to the lip of the well, and laid hold of the rope. The other man didn't appear to be tagging on to the end, so it had to be secured somewhere independently. A tree-trunk, probably.

Lemmon came down, hand over hand,

slowly. He was muttering and cursing to himself; he didn't like it down there. That increased my almost insane anger, my hatred for him. Only a devil could have put a human being down here to rot, a devil who was scared of his own medicine. The man was no more than a brute, an animal who well deserved to die. And within the next few minutes was going to.

I shifted my grip on the broken shaft, grasping it more firmly, keeping the blade below the water in case the light should catch it before I was ready. Now Lemmon was around six feet above me, still out of range.

He stopped his descent and called out, 'Where are you, Cane?' There was fear in his voice—not quite fear, though: more like horror, as though his flesh was crawling with the thought of slugs and other slimy weirdities, the things I'd had to put up with.

Still in that weak voice, though now I felt the strength of ten, I answered, 'Over here.'

He peered through the murk. I don't think he could actually see me yet, or anyway, not as any more than an outline.

He said, 'Right, stand up, then, if you can. Turn your back to me and I'll put the rope through your wrists like when you went down. Got it?'

'Yes,' I said.

He started coming down again. Five feet, four feet, three feet above the water, feet touching a moment later. He peered all around. 'Where the muckin' hell *are* you?'

'Right here,' I said. He was, in fact, looking directly at me in the moment I brought the scythe clear of the water and swung it towards him, strong and hard. I heard his furious cry of alarm, of terror, as the light from above caught the moving blade. He let go of the rope and dropped free.

The scythe caught the rope. There was no tension on that rope now, so it didn't even cut it. It just snagged it, and stopped its swing. There was no time for another go, no time to withdraw and swing again. I could have damn near cried. Lemmon, picking himself up from the water, surged towards me, grasping the shaft as he came and using it to force me back against the brickwork. Then his fist slammed into my face, once, twice, three times. The last thing I saw was his devilish face, and that scar, and the way the features were all twisted up, and then his fist coming at me again, and after that I passed out cold. When I came round I was in the dry, back in the cottage again, laying on the dirty, rotting boards and the bare earth, and Lemmon was there with the other man. The room swung around me and I felt seasick. My head was on fire, and my face too, and yet I was shivering as though I would never stop.

Lemmon and his friend seemed to gyrate, to swell to grotesque proportions and then shrink again. There was plenty of daylight, plenty of sun outside, and I could see their faces clearly enough. The other man was well-dressed, clean shaven, smooth and pale—somehow ascetic-looking. He was smiling, watching me pull through to searing pain and sickness, and I hated him as much as Lemmon.

'Well, well, Captain Cane,' he said in a light, easy voice, a cultured voice, but BBC English rather than upper class. 'God, but you gave some trouble down there, didn't you? I doubt if friend Lemmon's going to forgive you for that—eh, Lemmon?'

Lemmon used a series of obscenities.

'I don't like that language,' the man said sharply. 'There's no need for it and it doesn't help.' He came closer to me, and sniffed the air. 'The man still stinks,' he observed. 'I can't possibly have him in the car, Lemmon.'

'Well, that's up to you, innit?' Lemmon said. 'We can't leave him here and that's a mu—a fact.' He seemed a little in awe of the other man.

'Yes, yes, I know. You'll have to clean him up, that's all. Take him down to the lake and wash him, Lemmon. I'll cover you. Get his clothes off and rinse them through separately. We've got time in hand, but don't take *too* long over it.'

Lemmon started to argue. ''Snot all that important, is it? The car can be—'

'Do as you're told,' the man said. There was command and real authority in his voice. He was a big-timer, all right. 'I will not have filth in my car! Go on, get on with it.'

Lemmon scowled blackly but did as he'd been told. 'Get up,' he said to me roughly. He gave me a kick in the ribs and the man didn't stop him. I felt like very death, but when I saw the foot draw back again I did my best to move and after a spell of sick giddiness I lurched upright and clung to the wall for support. Lemmon said, 'Get moving.' He had had his gun in his hand all along, and now he jabbed it at me. I moved slowly for the door, feeling horribly ill, and saw that the other man also had a gun out now, an automatic. I went through the door and saw a car parked beyond the gate, a Daimler Jag, pointing towards the track all ready to move out once I was less smelly. I wondered where to; and wondered who the stranger was. Ottershaw? Could be, though he didn't strike me as an industrialist. More of an artist really, however unlikely. I went ahead, with the other two some paces behind me, and just after I had passed the Jag a voice said, 'Just a minute, if you don't mind,' and Chief Superintendent MacDown appeared from somewhere in the lee of the Jag with a heavy service revolver in his hand. I gave a weak cry of delight and surprise and relief, but, and I'll say this for him, Lemmon was quick in mind and body. He reacted on the instant. He was quite close to MacDown, as it happened, when the Chief Superintendent made his entrance, and he simply grabbed MacDown's skinny little body and flung it at me, revolver and all.

We both went down in a heap.

MacDown, cursing like a lunatic, recovered fast. He still had hold of his gun, and he fired towards the Jag, into which the two men were already scrambling. I was surprised they were beating it quite so readily. Return fire came back towards us, but missed. MacDown missed too. In its way—if I had been in any mood to appreciate it—it was quite a pantomime. MacDown was absolutely livid, even to the extent of blaming me for being in the way when he was thrown. He blazed away after the fast-moving Jag, quite uselessly, then threw down his revolver and jumped on it three or four times, not doing it any good at all.

I asked, 'How did you get here, Mr MacDown?'

'In a bloody car!' he snapped. 'How else d'you think?'

'Where is it?' I gazed around.

'Down the far side of the lake—I came the rest of the way on foot, to exploit the element of surprise.'

'Uh-huh,' I said with an unkindly inflexion. 'Will those two pass it on their way?'

'I expect they will,' MacDown said. 'We must hurry!' He paused, despite this hurry. 'What were they doing with you, Mr Cane?'

'I was being taken for a wash.'

He sniffed. 'Well, it'll have to wait—and you'll be going where I've come from—hospital. Come on, now.'

He started running; I hadn't the strength to follow. As MacDown belted off, I heard a fusilade of shots. 'Oh, damn and blast!' MacDown yelled in a frenzy. He almost tore at his hair. 'Now we'll need to walk!' He came back to me and handed me a brandy flask from his pocket. 'You'll need this,' he said.

Walk we did, with me much strengthened by the brandy; MacDown's car—an Austin Maxi that, he told me, he had hired to replace the Humber—had all its tyres shot flat and a few bullet holes in the bonnet as well, plus a shattered windscreen. There was no sign of the two men or the Jag and I wondered again why they were just leaving us to it rather than trying to get hold of us and doing to us both whatever it was they had intended to do to me.

I asked MacDown about that.

'Panic,' he said briefly. 'They didn't think.'

I said, 'I'd doubt that. They aren't the sort.'

'Then maybe they don't want to stick their necks out so far as to kidnap *me.*'

I looked at him. 'Do they know who you are, then?'

'I can't say,' he said, shrugging. 'It's possible they do, and if they do, well, there's more reason for panic. Come along, now.' I was staggering about like a drunk. 'Hold on till we reach the village, then we'll get transport. It's not all that far.'

'How far?'

'I don't know,' Macdown said; obviously he did, but didn't want to depress me. 'As I said—not far.'

We plodded on, up a very steep track. I said, 'I wonder who the other man was, Lemmon's friend. Ottershaw, d'you think?'

'Not Ottershaw.'

'How d'you know? Do you know Ottershaw?'

'I've seen photographs of the man. It's not him, definitely not.'

'Who is he, then?'

MacDown said snappishly, 'I don't

know, Mr Cane, I don't know.' He was still feeling bitter and really I wasn't all that surprised. To come in for an arrest and lose not only your villains but your hired car as well, isn't a happy thing for a police officer of high rank. He'd boobed and he knew it; he should have come in with a show of strength, a whole platoon of cops. But then, of course, he wasn't an *ordinary* cop any more, and there could be invisible difficulties His branch were a law unto themselves. I asked him how he had found out about the cottage.

'Ways,' he said obliquely. 'Ways and means. You see, when you failed to come and see me in the hospital again, I began to worry, Mr Cane. You are not an experienced man, and you would, I was well aware, have needed to seek my advice fairly continuously. Unless, that was, you were unable to do so. Thus it occurred to me that something had gone wrong, and I made discreet enquiries by telephone from my room. Then the Humber was found abandoned, and there were sundry fingerprints...to cut a long story short, I decided it was time to forget what Mr Limbrick had said about keeping all this within the family. Not too far outside it, however. Just a wee way, that's all. At times, and within limits, the local forces have their good uses. Suffice it, Mr Crane, to say this much: the Humber's movements were traced. This is not entirely deserted countryside, whatever Lemmon and his superiors may like to think. Remember, you have been missing for three full days. When I had enough to go upon, I left hospital.

'With the doctors' blessings?'

'No. I discharged myself. They were pretty angry, but they had to lump it. The leg is perfectly well now.'

I didn't think it was, since he was limping now and again, and his face was a little pinched, but it was his concern after all. As for me, I didn't feel able to move another step, but I kept going because I damn well had to. I couldn't wait to see a nice inhabited village again, anyway. So I stumbled on, through waves of weariness and nausea and my own stench, and MacDown gave me another suck at his brandy flask, and while we were stopped for this, and for MacDown to screw the cap back on again, I saw a movement ahead behind one of those low stone walls, just on a bend. I said, 'Mr

MacDown, a little while ago you spoke about panic and discretion, about those men not wanting to stick their necks out too far.'

'What are you on about now?' MacDown asked irritably.

'Don't look now, but I think you were wrong on both counts.'

'Why?'

I said, 'Because I think they're waiting for us ahead.'

MacDown drew in his breath sharply and murmured, 'Oh, Jesus Christ.' I dare say he was feeling as naked as I. I waited for him to pronounce on whether we tried to scarper out of sight across country, or whether we battled through behind his heavy revolver.

CHAPTER SIX

'Well, which?' I asked; and MacDown gave me the answer I had expected him to give and in pretty much the exact words too.

'Discretion is the better part of valour,' he said, 'though we're going to be dead lucky if we get away with it, Mr Cane. Follow me.'

I did. MacDown plunged through a gap in the dry-stone wall and kept low, and I reeled along behind. On the other side of the wall, way ahead around a bend in the track, I saw the Jag's roof. I couldn't see Lemmon and the other man just then, and I hoped without much conviction that they couldn't see us. I was not quite sure what MacDown had in mind to do, and I hadn't the breath to ask him, for he was moving in a fast crouch along the inside of the wall, heading, I think, for a belt of trees that reached almost to the wall itself. I had my doubts that he would simply run for out and try to rustle up some assistance; he wasn't the type for that. There was a curious tenacity about him, and an obstinacy; he probably wouldn't like being bettered. I fancied his plan would probably be to outflank those two and come up in the rear, whatever he had said about discretion, and then attempt to make an arrest. If so, I hoped his shooting would be a little more accurate than it had been earlier.

We reached the trees. I still hadn't seen

the men, but the Jag hadn't moved and was still visible. MacDown began working up to the left once we were in the trees, keeping nicely hidden and making very little sound. The trees led around towards the Jag, and I wondered if he meant to immobilize it before trying to make his arrest. It might be a sensible thing to do, to cut off the retreat, but I cursed to myself because it would mean a continuance of this wretched walk and I knew I was reaching the end of my endurance, but fast.

I needn't have worried. All through, we hadn't really had much of a chance and now history, in a sense, repeated itself in reverse. From a bush a little ahead of MacDown's stealthy progress a mocking voice said, 'Just a minute...if you don't muckin' mind,' and Lemmon emerged with his gun aimed at MacDown's guts. From the other side, Lemmon's boss came out with *his* gun pointing at me.

Lemmon said, 'Let's have your gun, copper.'

'Now look here, Lemmon, just see sense–'

'I won't tell you again. We don't have all day.' Lemmon gestured with his gun.

'Nobody's goin' to hear when I blow your gut through your backbone.'

MacDown shrugged. Sententiously he said, 'He who fights and runs away, lives to fight another day.'

'Does he?' Lemmon's boss asked pleasantly. 'Nice for him. I doubt if that's going to apply to you, though. The gun, if you please.'

MacDown handed it over. Lemmon moved behind him; the other man moved behind me and I felt his gun in my back. 'March out, Captain Cane,' he said, still sounding pleasant. We moved ahead and came clear of the trees. Four minutes later we were in the Jag, with Lemmon driving and the boss keeping MacDown and me covered. Lemmon went up a steep climb, heading for the main road intersection, where he turned left along the A684 towards Hawes and Kendal. We were back in that magnificent Dales scenery again, hurtling dangerously along beneath the Pennine peaks, but I wasn't watching the scenery. I was listening, with interest and some admiration, to Chief Superintendent MacDown.

You would never have thought he was the captured party.

He was treating those two as though he had arrested them and, in his own way, was actually conducting an investigation. It was pretty amazing, and Lemmon's boss, though not Lemmon himself, was amused enough to play along with MacDown—a fact that I found singularly indicative of potential danger for MacDown and me. But then I'd been expecting to die for quite some time now, so I suppose the situation hadn't really changed.

MacDown started off by attacking Lemmon. 'Frank Peter Archibald Lemmon,' he said as though reading out the charge sheet, 'specialist in robbing churches and cathedrals of valuable plate. A shocking thing—sacrilege. However, there's worse. On the 14th April three years since, you raped and murdered a young woman, a schoolgirl, in the Metropolitan Police area. Have you anything to say?'

'Yes,' Lemmon said.

'Then go on.'

'Get stuffed,' Lemmon said, 'good and hard.'

MacDown merely nodded. 'I expected something of the sort from a young tearaway like you,' he observed quietly. 'However, you will shortly be charged with that crime, make no mistake about it.' I knew he was bluffing and of course Lemmon knew it too, but MacDown sounded confident enough. 'There will now be additions to the charge. Abduction, violence, causing actual bodily harm, attempted murder, being concerned with other persons in an attempt to pervert the course of government...and I think you'll know, Lemmon, precisely what I mean by that?'

'Do I?' Lemmon's face was blank, watching out ahead as he handled the Jag expertly around the bends. 'Just in case I don't, you can tell me all about it, in your own muckin' words.'

'All in good time,' MacDown said. He shifted comfortably in his seat, stretching out his legs. He was utterly at ease and in a curious way was in command. 'Now, another matter. Who is this man?' He indicated Lemmon's boss.

'Ask him,' Lemmon said.

MacDown nodded, and turned an enquiring face on the man. 'Well?'

The man laughed. 'I don't see why you shouldn't know. It won't convey anything. I haven't any—what d'you call it in your jargon—form, isn't it?'

134

'Form is correct,' Macdown said. 'And you have none?'

'None at all.'

MacDown smiled. 'As innocent as a new-born baby. And your name?'

'Darnley. In full—Paul Redvers Darnley, of Bolton, Lancashire.'

'Oh, no, it isn't,' MacDown said. There was a crafty look in his eye and complacency in his voice, and he was as perky as a sparrow. He had dropped a bomb and of course he knew it. The car swerved a little as Lemmon reacted, then steadied. The other man, less pleasant now, demanded, 'What the devil d'you mean by that?'

'What I say,' MacDown answered. 'You are Horace Peacock and you have served more than one term of imprisonment, the last being in the Moor. It was, I think, seven years. You will remember what the crime was, of course.'

'I don't know what you're talking about,' the man said; but he did, and even I could see it. There was fear and fury in his eyes. I don't know how he had done it, but MacDown had hit the target dead centre.

MacDown smiled and caught my eye.

'The crime was blackmail,' he said calmly. 'Blackmail, and using threats of, and carrying out, physical violence. Mr Cane, I think we are getting somewhere.' He looked at the man he had said was Horace Peacock. 'Would you not agree?'

The man licked at his lips. 'What makes you say all this?' he demanded hoarsely. 'I just don't understand.'

MacDown said, 'I have an infallible memory for *voices*, Peacock. Your appearance has changed a very great deal—I do indeed congratulate you, for it's clever enough—but the moment I heard you speak I recognised Horace Peacock. You find that astonishing?'

'I've never seen you before in my life,' Peacock said.

'Possibly not. You were not my case, I will admit—I didn't arrest you. But I was in court, and your case was a long one. Blackmail has always been my main interest, Peacock. I have made it my business to attend *all* the big blackmail hearings. As a matter of fact, it's because of this speciality of mine that I have been assigned to this current investigation. And I might add that your name was on my list of possibles from the start.' He paused, and cleared his throat. 'Do you not think, Peacock, that you should tell me all about it now?'

A remarkable performance on MacDown's part, considering his present situation; but it ended there. Horace Peacock's face suddenly suffused and he struck out at MacDown with his automatic, bringing it crashing down on his temple. MacDown went out like a light and blood poured into his eyes. He looked small and lonely and pathetic.

I thought MacDown had been foolishly precipitate, that he would have done far better to have hung on to his private knowledge and make use of it in some other way and at some other time; but of course he did know his job. (I realized later, a long while after we had reached the end of that journey, that he had done the right thing. He had taken due account of the fact that an attribute shared by the majority of villains like Peacock is a tendency to boast. They just can't conceal how clever they have been, and the more involved the crime, the more they like to gloat. That is, when they feel dead safe to do so. Peacock evidently did feel dead safe and so, like any other peacock, he strutted).

Journey's end this time was in a back street in Kendal, where we pulled into a small builder's yard—that was what it looked like, anyway—adjoining an end-of-terrace house, small and dingy, with the neighbour's washing blowing on a keen wind over the fence at the back. It didn't seem to me the right and proper setting for big-time crime and Peacock himself obviously came from a very different background. As a matter of fact I found out later that he had been at Oundle and Cambridge, which had a certain significance. And I do mean within the context of the case. Anyway, we were ushered into the kitchen of this house in front of concealed guns—MacDown had recovered by now, but he still looked white and shaken, and his leg seemed to be bothering him again. We were told to go through the kitchen, which we did, and we entered what I suppose was the front parlour, a dreadful room, all plush and velvet and a horrible orange carpet surrounded by lino, and a cottage piano. Over the fireplace were two huge photographs in very ornately decorated frames and these were of, believe it or not, Queen Victoria and Mr Gladstone, a juxtaposition that would have pleased neither of them in life. But there was also a settee, or possibly it was a *chaise-longue;* I went for it and lay down flat. I don't know what Peacock or Lemmon thought, or Clapp who was also in that room waiting for us; and I didn't care. I didn't know a thing for a long time afterwards, because I just went out. I went into a terrible nightmare; I couldn't breathe and I was bathed in sweat and I was back in that stinking well and the slugs were coming for me, huge and fat and slimy, and settling on my mouth and nostrils so that with each attempt to breathe I filled my air passages with those softly yielding bodies. I had no idea how long I sayed like that but when at last I awoke I was in a bed, not a very clean one as I discovered later, and Lemmon was standing by with his arms folded, and another man, a stranger, was prodding at me and talking away in a low voice.

When I opened my eyes he seemed pleased, and gave a series of nods. To Lemmon he said, 'Yes, I think I can safely say the worst is over. He'll pull through now. Wonderful stuff, these antibiotics, I don't know *what* we'd do without them. I gave him something really strong.' He paused. 'Is Mr Darnley in?'

'Out,' Lemmon said briefly.

'Well, if you'll just tell him all's well. Carry on with the nursing. It—er—might be better if I didn't call again, don't you think? Get him up in forty-eight hours.' The man nodded and smiled and went out of the room.

'Who was that?' I asked.

'Doctor, who d'you think?'

'A bent one, I somehow gathered. Why are you taking so much trouble to keep me alive, Lemmon?'

'You'll find out,' Lemmon said vindictively.

'How's Mr MacDown?'

'Alive,' Lemmon said, sitting down in an easy chair. 'Now shut up. I have to guard you, but I don't have to listen to you. Unless you want to say anythin' worth hearin', that is.'

'Such as what?'

Lemmon got up again and lounged across to my bedside. He folded his arms like before and stood there looking down on me, his scar and pimples standing out like red wax. 'Such as what you were doing in Drayling churchyard,' he said.

'Oh. That again. No, thanks, not today.'

'And such as what you took from that muckin' vault.'

I stared; this was new. I said, 'I didn't take anything. I don't understand you. Is anything missing?'

Lemmon stared back at me, then said flatly, 'The boss'll be talking to you soon,' and went back to his on guard position. He walked with his hands dangling, and for the first time I realized how immensely long his arms were, just like an ape. Soon after this Horace Peacock came in and asked me how I felt.

'Better,' I said.

'That's good. You can start giving me the answers to some questions. God knows, I've had to wait long enough.' He pulled an upright chair across and planted it by the head of the bed, and sat with his own face close to mine. 'To start with—'

'Hang on,' I said, feeling a sudden sense of time running out. 'How long have I been out?'

'Two days.'

I did a quick sum in my head. Two plus three plus two—something like that—that made seven. Add a day for Drayling, and I fancied we had just two days left before the House of Commons voted on that Corporation Tax motion. Something had to come to a head before then or the Government Whips were going to be given some highly unexpected instructions. I saw Peacock looking at me and smiling broadly. 'Does the sum work out?' he asked.

'Is that a sort of admission?'

He lifted an eyebrow. 'Of what, Captain Cane?'

I said, 'Shall we stop fencing? It's gone on rather a long time now. Chief Superintendent MacDown has already bowled you out and I don't see you're gaining anything at all by going on pretending now.'

He nodded, not at all put out. He seemed to have got his confidence back, since that performance by MacDown. 'Well, yes, I suppose that's true. All right, Cane. We'll all come into the open, shall we? A certain division is due to take place down in Westminster shortly, and I think we both know what about. I think we both know what may happen, and why, so we'll take that as read, all right?'

'You *are* making an admission, aren't you?'

'Call it what you like, it's not really important to me. As a matter of fact it won't be important to you either, unless you help me, Cane. I think you know what I mean by that.'

'Sure I know,' I said. Then I added, 'We know what you're up to, and so do some other people that you've *not* landed in your net, and *you'll know what I* mean by that. I've no doubt you think you've been bloody clever, Peacock, but in point of fact you're on a very poor wicket right now.'

It was bluff, of course; and it didn't come off. Peacock just laughed, quite indulgently, and it was then that he spread his colourful tail for me to admire. Good old Macdown had triggered if off back along the road to Kendal and now Peacock was in full squawk. He had nothing to lose now, and even a much less vain man would hardly have held back. And in its way it really was clever. To start with, the basics were precisely as known: the Prime Minister had been threatened with exposure of his Ministerial protégé, Harold Marton, unless he gave certain specific directions to his Whips. The Prime

Minister was very well aware indeed of what exposure could, and would, do to his own position and that of his party. He faced disaster, naturally. He had not yet indicated what course he was going to take, but Peacock regarded this as a foregone conclusion.

'Unless,' I said, 'the negatives are found and destroyed, or rather held by the police, before the division takes place.'

'Ah yes—quite! But that's not going to happen...is it?'

'How do you mean?' I was puzzled. After all, I thought, why ask me?

'Come on,' Peacock said, and there was an edge to his voice now. 'Don't play around with me, please. I don't need to keep stressing the fact that you're in my hands and are not going to get out—do I?'

'No, no,' I said. 'Point taken. But I don't think you've told me all yet, have you? Where do you fit? Were you the concealed photographer—or was it Ottershaw?'

He smiled. 'It wasn't Ottershaw. That's definite. In any case, I know Ottershaw. A crude man, an industrialist—enough said, I think! No finesse, no imagination. A bludgeon, whereas this is work for a rapier.

For a man of keen mind.'

'Like you?'

He grinned. 'I blush! Look, Cane...why don't you face the inevitable and tell me who's side you're on, apart from your own, that is?'

I didn't understand, but I countered it. I said, 'Why don't you just tell me the whole story first?'

He looked at me and frowned; I believe he himself was puzzled just then. He said as if to himself, 'Sort of fill in the gaps, eh...well, I suppose it's logical to accept that you can't really know the *whole* story.' I didn't comment, in case I should say the wrong thing, the thing that would turn off what I felt was to be the flow. It was. He seemed to come to a decision and went on, 'All right, then. You'll have to forgive me when I come to the parts you're familiar with. It'd be better if I gave you it all right through more or less in sequence. After that...well, I hope we can come to some satisfactory arrangement.'

'I hope so,' I said, still in the dark.

He frowned again, then leaned closer to me. He said, 'The strange thing is, and this you have to believe, I don't know who *did* take those photographs.

All I know is—they were sent through the post to Ottershaw. The prints, that is. The package was opened by his confidential secretary. It so happens I'm on very good terms with her and she told me. The prints were accompanied by an anonymous typewritten note suggesting what Ottershaw could achieve with them if he felt inclined, and a promise that the negatives would be handed over to him at a certain place and time in exchange for ten thousand pounds in used one-pound notes. The writer obviously knew the man he was dealing with. Well, to cut a longish story down to essentials, Ottershaw decided to buy, and he turned up at the rendezvous. He handed over the cash and was given the negatives.

'You're sure of this?'

'Of course I'm sure. We weren't watching the rendezvous—too dangerous—but on the way back afterwards, Ottershaw met with an accident—he was driving alone, for obvious reasons. The cause of the accident was our friend Lemmon, assisted by Clapp and Phillips. They brought the negatives to me. Which left Ottershaw ten thousand quid worse off and nothing to show for it. He must have been livid, but there was nothing he could do about it—well, I mean, he could hardly go to the police, could he?'

I agreed with that. 'What did you do with the negatives?' I asked. 'Was it you who sent prints to the Prime Minister?'

'It was. But that's only half the story, isn't it? D'you want me to go on?'

'Please do,' I said, and again I had a strong feeling he was highly puzzled about me.

He said, 'Personally, I don't give a hoot about Corporation Tax—I don't pay it, so why should I worry? I even manage to minimize my own income tax problems quite satisfactorily! But, you see, old Ottershaw is *known* to detest Corporation Tax to the point of insanity—and if his secretary cares to corroborate, he'll be known to have had that suggestion put to him, and he'll be known to have accepted it lock, stock and barrel. Now do you see?'

I said, 'I'm getting there. Quite fast. After the deed is done—after the Government has lost that division—Ottershaw can be dropped in the creek. By you. Unless he, I suppose, pays you a sum of money?'

'Brilliant!' Peacock said, giving me a little handclap. 'A hundred thousand quid to be exact. Clever—yes?'

I had to agree. Sordid, but clever. 'There's one thing bothering me,' I said. 'Why did Ottershaw go and stay with the Martons at Drayling? Don't tell me that was sheer chance!'

'Of course it wasn't, as well you know.'

'*I* know?'.'

Peacock said patiently, 'Now look. It was you who suggested we should stop fencing, Cane, old man. Why not follow your own good idea?' He added, 'I'm not really grasping, and if there's no need to do you an injury, well, I won't do you one. A hundred thou is a lot of money, even today. Also, I'm confident Ottershaw can be made to yield more over the happy, profitable years ahead. I certainly won't grudge you your share, even if you don't damn well deserve it. Without the negatives to back me up, I can't do a damn thing, as you obviously realize. Those negatives...they're the final, absolute guarantee that I can back threats with action.'

I said, 'You're way ahead of me, I'm afraid. I take it you're saying you've lost

148

the negatives. What d'you expect me to do about that?'

His patience snapped, then. He almost shouted his next words at me. 'Tell me where the bloody things are, what else!'

CHAPTER SEVEN

Not unnaturally, I think, my reaction was a peal of laughter. Peacock didn't like that; neither did Lemmon. Lemmon came across to the bed and told me to shut up or I would be sorry. I stopped laughing and said, 'Well, what else do you expect me to do? You don't really *mean* that about the negatives, do you, Peacock?'

'You know very well I'm not joking.'

I nodded, studying his face. 'Yes, I rather think I do. But really, you have got things a little twisted. If I'd ever had my hands on those negatives, they'd be at Downing Street right now. Or Scotland Yard.'

'And they're not?'

'No,' I said, and could have bitten off my tongue the moment I'd spoken. In fact I should have bitten it off earlier; I'd missed a wonderful opportunity of putting the wind right up Peacock where it would inflate most. My God, I'd boobed! He'd handed it all to me on a plate, which made my gall the more bitter—or so I thought until he opened his mouth again, and then I saw that things were not quite as they had seemed.

Peacock said with a hard laugh, 'I didn't imagine they would be in official hands, somehow. You'd better begin to realize your position, Cane. You're not going to get away from here, you know. If you talk, you can make all the difference to your life. Can't you see the game's up?'

I stared at him; I was ticking over a shade faster now, and I said, 'Somebody, somewhere, has his wires crossed pretty badly. Why not clear both our minds, and tell me just who and what you believe I am?'

I saw that puzzled frown again, and the way Peacock met Lemmon's eye with a query in his expression. Lemmon gave a small shrug and looked baffled too. Peacock, asked, 'Are you saying you're genuinely a Special Branch man?'

'Of a kind,' I said. 'Temporary acting.

I dare say I leave a lot to be desired in the performance of my duties, but I do my best. Why do you ask?'

'Because we think you're not,' Peacock answered flatly. 'We think you're working for another party—maybe for Ottershaw himself. Or even just for *your*self. Whatever you say, we still believe that, Cane. Even Limbrick could be behind it. Look at it this way. You get taken on by Limbrick, just at the drop of a hat—and don't ask how I know, the fact remains I *do*. Army background—okay, so what? It doesn't qualify you for a police job, not without plenty of training first. MacDown we know. He's straight, a real career copper. The bloodhound breed. Nothing would ever deflect *him*. Limbrick's different, so are you.'

'What are you suggesting?' I asked.

Peacock said, 'That Limbrick's bent. You too. That's why he hired you, why he put you up for interview. He's a big man, is Limbrick. He gets his way.'

I said, 'It's fantastic, mad, crazy.'

Peacock shook his head. 'Oh no, it isn't. Things happen that way. At the bottom of the scale, you get coppers pinched for supermarket lifting, or men on the beat doing a spot of breaking-and-entering in the dark and silent hours. You know that. Very few, I'll agree—but it happens! So why not at the top?'

'Too much to lose,' I said.

'Comparatively, no more than a constable. A constable stands to lose say twelve hundred a year and a nice pension. To a constable's standard of living as compared to Limbrick's, that equivalent to Limbrick's loss if he gets caught out. But the difference is that in Limbrick's case the actual stakes are sky-high and well worth the risk. They're not packets of peas from Tesco. With those negatives in his pocket, he could make himself almost a millionaire—and he's got all the cast-iron opportunities for hopping the twig out of the country before he puts the squeeze on. But I'll bet the cut he's giving you isn't all that big, and I think I can cap it. All you have to do, is tell me where the negatives are.'

I said, 'You're crazy. You're all wrong about Limbrick.' But even as I said it, I had started to wonder. Limbrick was a curious customer in a way, and I *had* been hired, if not at the drop of a hat, virtually at the drop of a large scotch. It made one think. But really it was all much too fantastic for me; and I had an idea this Peacock could have had his brain turned a fraction, that he had indeed gone a little round the bend with the thought of all the riches to come and that this was why he was having these lunatic ideas about me and Limbrick. I went on, 'You're definitely wrong about me, Peacock. I'm on the level. I'm not double-crossing anybody, and I don't work for Ottershaw or anyone else, just the Monarch, that's all.'

He nodded, but he was still disbelieving. 'Think about it,' he advised. 'Think about it well—but remember there's not much time left.'

'If there's not much time left, why waste what there is? By concentrating on me, that's just what you are doing, not that I care. All I'm supposed to care about, is stopping your blackmail plan going through. If you put the block on yourself, why should MacDown or I bother our heads about it?' Then—very suddenly—something hit me. Hard, in a mental sense. Drayling churchyard, and Lemmon and Clapp, and the gunnery with me behind the tombstones. And the fresh cement on the grille. I said, 'That vault.

153

You know—the Marton vault.'

'Exactly,' Peacock said. There was excitement and relief on his face now, and in Lemmon's too. 'Come on, Cane!'

'Just a moment,' I said. 'It sounds mad, but were the negatives in there—and do *you* think I was there to pinch them?'

'Weren't you?'

I said, 'Answer my question, Peacock. Were the negatives there?'

He gave an evil sort of grin, more of a grimace. 'God, you're persistent! You know damn well they were there—and if you're wondering why, the answer is they had to go somewhere and they were too hot to keep on anyone's person or anyone's property. So why not the dead? Who'd ever think of looking in Drayling, of all places? And who'd ever think of looking in a coffin...except perhaps Ottershaw or his stooge?'

I said, 'Oh, come on, let's get this straight! I thought I was Limbrick's stooge, wasn't I?'

'I'm only speculating. I have to admit that, Cane. You could still be working for Ottershaw. Ottershaw could have got the word—money talks, Cane. If that's the case, and if I ever find out who did talk, that man's going to be sorry he was ever born. But that's for the future. The fact remains that Ottershaw was at Drayling Hall, staying with the Martons, and then you turned up, and when we checked, the negatives had gone. I think you'd better start talking in real earnest, Cane, or you're not going to live much longer. That's a promise. So is something else.'

'What?'

'Two other people are going to have a little attention paid to them. Your friends in Drayling. The Crimonds. As a matter of fact, their cottage is going to be done over this evening—unless you talk before then.'

Peacock had left me soon after that, and Clapp the skinhead had taken over guard duty from Lemmon. My head was in a whirl; everything was crazy. It was impossible to convince Peacock that I knew nothing about those negatives, and his own theories were as mixed as all hell. If I didn't know where I stood, or currently lay, then neither did he. He was torn between Limbrick, and Ottershaw, and possibly other parties unknown. His one fixed certainty was that I was as bent as a safety-pin, and he was wrong on that too, poor chap. He'd made a proper balls, but that was no help to me now. I was firmly in his hands, without a doubt, and I was dead worried about Bill and Eve Crimond. Quite apart from what might happen to *them*—and Peacock had uttered that very definite threat—I hated to think of that little cottage being all broken up, desecrated by low-life bastards like Lemmon and Clapp and Phillips. Then there were the children. I remembered Lemmon's record and I shuddered. The Crimonds' children were a good deal younger than the girl Lemmon had murdered, but a brute like Lemmon wouldn't have any lines to draw. I watched Clapp's tight face and thin slit of a mouth as he read a paperback with a naked girl on the cover, saw him now and again lift a hand to scratch his scalp, visible all over through the cropped hair. On that hand were four heavy metal rings—cheap, trashy jewellery with a dirty purpose behind it. It would be difficult for the police to prove that they constituted an offensive weapon. On those grounds, my old grandmother would have qualified for the nick.

Clapp's legs were thrust into heavy nailed boots—bovver boots I suppose they were. They looked horrible and ugly and menacing. I kept on thinking of a similar boot smashing into Eve's face. If I'd happened to have known where the negatives were, I'd have sent word to Peacock to come back up and I'd have told him, gladly. And the Prime Minister, and the Government, and Limbrick, could all get flaming well knackered. In my view, a personal friendship, and the protection of the innocent when you can, is a damn sight more important than disembodied concepts of democracy and more important by far than the preservation of the sanctified pomposity of any Prime Minister who ever sat in the study at No 10. And I swore two things to myself that day: one, that I was going to save the Crimonds from the beat-up boys whatever happened to those wretched negatives, for this thing had now become personal; and two, when this job was over, Limbrick could go to hell. I wasn't taking part in any more such missions. I would rather sell insurance.

In the meantime, something had to be thought up.

But what?

First things first, I thought. Consider the objective: I had to get away from this house, away from Kendal, and I had to have transport. Or at least I had to get to a police station and have word telephoned south, word that would send a strong squad out to Drayling from Huntingdon to protect Bill and Eve Crimond. This would mean breaking faith with Limbrick, but I didn't care now.

There could, of course, be one way to do this—the only way, it seemed to me. It was chancy, and it could be difficult to convince Peacock that I was telling the truth, but it had to be tried. At the very least it ought to diminish the personnel here in this house, and with luck it might get me out in the open.

I called to Clapp, and he looked up from his paperback. I said, 'I want a word with Peacock.'

'What about?'

'What he wanted,' I said.

Clapp gave me a hard look and, still watching me, backed to the door and shouted down the stairs. Peacock was up in five seconds flat. 'Well?' he asked.

I said, 'All right, you win.'

'Where are the negatives?'

158

'I'm coming to that, but I'll want some safeguards first.'

'You can have all the safeguards you want, Cane.'

'Fine,' I said. 'First, the Crimonds. They're to be left alone—they can't help you anyway. Second, MacDown's not to be hurt in any way at all and he's to be released just as soon as it's safe. Third,' I added, because this had to be convincing, 'there's my cut. I want fifty per cent of all proceeds, and that includes anything you get out of Ottershaw in the future, whenever you decide to squeeze him.'

He agreed at once, too readily. 'Now tell me,' he said, 'where I'll find the negatives?'

I said, 'Not so fast, Peacock. I want some real assurance that my cut's safe. I like cash in the bank.'

'Not possible,' he said. 'This thing has to be handled discreetly. No big sums all at once. In any case I can't pay out till Ottershaw coughs up.'

I said, 'No, that's understood. I still want the assurance, though, and this is how it'll be done. I'm not *telling* you where the negatives are hidden. I'm going to take you there myself.'

'But—'

'No buts,' I said. 'Take it or leave it, Peacock.'

He was clearly agog with excitement and he caved in; he became co-operative. 'Okay. And then?'

'You and I will put them into a sealed envelope with my name on it. That envelope will go into another envelope with a covering letter, which I'll sign, addressed to my bank manager in London. The inner envelope, the one with the negatives, will be held for me by my bank. You'll have seen for yourself that what you want is in it. We'll drop it in the post together, but only I can get it out again. You agree to that?'

He nodded. 'Yes, I do. I'll accompany you to your bank, of course, when you withdraw the envelope.'

'That's all right by me,' I said, 'just so long as I get my cut in the end, Peacock.'

'You will,' he assured me.

'And just so long as you draw your tearaways right off the Crimonds and leave them strictly alone, remember?'

'You have my promise,' Peacock said, and I didn't believe him for one moment.

I knew he wouldn't be leaving anything uncovered from now on out and he still needed a lever against me. He didn't say any more after that, he just gestured to Clapp to stay on guard and he went downstairs again. For a moment I heard his voice, though I couldn't hear what he said, and then a door slammed. He came back soon after with notepaper and I wrote the letter to my bank. Then I was left in peace. I wondered where poor old MacDown was, and what he would have thought of the way I was handling things. I started to work the details out in my mind, how I was to get away from Peacock and the others when the time came, where it would be best to lead them on the forthcoming wild goose chase for the negatives. I also wondered where on earth the negatives really were; somebody had to have them! The fact they existed could still give rise to some surprises for all concerned, and I could only hope their current owners wouldn't go into action before we got on the phony track—if that happened, I would be right up the creek and no paddles handy. But it was a chance I had to take, though as the day wore on it seemed a worse and worse chance since if time was running out for Peacock it was also running out for the man who really did have the negatives and he wouldn't be wasting his opportunities. However, all I could do was to be constructive, which for now meant planning that hiding place. I thought it had better be somewhere not too far off Drayling, for that would not only appear reasonable to Peacock if he thought I had hidden them after being disturbed by Lemmon, but it would also position me near the Crimonds. And there was a public call box in the village, I seemed to remember, and a resident country copper.

The more I thought about it, the more I fancied Drayling itself as the supposed dump. Then I recollected something pretty important: the cement around the grille. New it had been, certainly, but not freshly set, not *wet*. If Lemmon and his pals had been there to bring out the negatives, they couldn't possibly have missed that. They weren't that daft, I assumed. At least, I couldn't take the risk. So I could hardly claim to have nicked the negatives on that occasion. If asked, I would have to say I'd gone back on the chance of finding more, something of that sort, but had been bowled out too soon by Lemmon.

So where?

Boroughbridge! It was a long way from Bill's cottage but it was logical enough and there, too, I would have a call box handy. Yes—Boroughbridge. But not my room at the hotel, for there was a strong chance Peacock would already have found a way of going through my things there and once he got the idea that that was where we were heading, he would call the project off.

That was when I had the bright idea: MacDown's mantrap episode. It wasn't quite Boroughbridge, but it would do quite nicely. No one would ever have found anything in the forest, and I would have had the opportunity of getting rid of the evidence safely and securely while MacDown had been nipped like a rabbit in a snare and yelling out his oaths. I thought it would hold water, but I was going to need to do some fast thinking and moving when we reached the area.

When Peacock came back he said he was ready to move out any time now. 'How far do we have to go?' he asked.

'Not too far. Say around seventy miles. I don't think it's more.' I saw him trying to work it out, taking a radius all around and no doubt seeing somewhere around Boroughbridge way as the likely area. I said, 'I'm ready when you are, though that tame doctor of yours did say I was to keep in bed for a couple of days. I'd advise waiting till it's dark, all the same.'

'Yes,' Peacock said. 'We'll get into the area after dark, but there's no reason why we shouldn't start off from here while it's light. Seventy miles, you say. Well, you can lie up and get some sleep till eight o'clock tonight. Then we move out, all right?'

I nodded. 'That suits me. Just so long as you keep to your part of the bargain. For that, I have to trust you. But just bear this in mind, Peacock: if anything happens to Major and Mrs Crimond, or Mr MacDown, that envelope doesn't come out of my bank. You need me for that extraction, Peacock.'

'I know,' he said, and smiled. 'You needn't worry. Your friends don't really interest me, so long as I get what I want from you. The moment you produce the negatives, they're safe.'

Which was precisely my worry, since I wasn't going to produce any negatives. But there was nothing I could do about it at the moment. I was doing the best I could and I would just have to hope everything turned out well. Once again Peacock left me and I didn't see him again until close to the time for moving out. The guard on me was changed periodically, and meals were brought. I felt fairly fit, considering, and I managed to eat quite well. During the afternoon a strange face appeared, and I gathered this was Phillips, the third of the trio, the man who had shot at me out of the dark in Drayling churchyard. Like Clapp, he was a close-cropped, bovver-booted skinhead. He had a thoroughly sadistic face and when he sat down watchfully, he placed a docker's cargo-hook on the arm of the chair beside him. It was a nasty looking weapon, very shiny and needle-pointed. It could, I knew, draw out a man's throat like a winkle coming out of its shell on the end of a pin.

I felt shaky when I got up, very weak at the knees, and I had an attack of giddiness, but this passed off. Peacock gave me a large, stiff whisky and this helped a lot. I asked him for a flask for the journey; I had to keep on the ball right the way along the line now. He agreed to that, and before we went out to the Jag he handed me a half-bottle-size pewter flask. 'That ought to keep you going,' he said. 'I'm putting you in front with Lemmon. He's driving. You can guide him. I'll be in the back with Phillips. Clapp stays behind, in charge.'

He didn't utter any threats, but I got the idea. As a matter of fact, he was being quite friendly now, really matey, but I didn't make the mistake of imagining he was trusting me. We went out to the car and got in and Lemmon asked for his first directions. I said, 'Take the road through the Dales, the one we came on. By the way, where's MacDown?'

Peacock said, 'Don't worry about him, he's all right, only we don't want him in on this, do we?'

'No, I suppose not. Remember he's part of the bargain, though. He's not to be roughed up.'

'He won't be.'

Lemmon asked, 'Do we go all the way, Mister Cane?'

I said, 'For a start, let's say as far as Hawes, shall we? After that, I'll give you another reference.'

In the back, Peacock laughed. 'Quite the

mystery man,' he said. 'Like to keep us guessing, eh?'

I turned and smiled at him. 'I don't suppose there's much point, but it makes it more interesting.'

'You mean you don't want us to jump to any conclusions ahead of you,' he said with another laugh. 'Well, never mind, so long as we get what we're going for. I don't suppose I need go into any details as to what'll happen if anything goes wrong, Cane.'

Peacock sat back, and carried on a desultory conversation with Phillips, who still had his cargo-hook handy. We went out fast for Hawes, through the evening light. We passed through Sedbergh. The Dales were magnificent as the light began to fade behind the peaks to the west. Soon, as we left Hawes, still on the same road for West Witton and Leyburn, the odd pinpoint of light appeared in the scattered, isolated farms and cottages. We didn't in fact go into Leyburn; in Wensley I saw a sign to Masham, which was on the road to Ripon, so I told Lemmon to turn off there, and we went fast through Masham and then Ripon, where I put Lemmon on the track for

Carnforth House, Ottershaw's place. In the back, Peacock grew restive. I think he had guessed the precise destination now, and I had no doubt he was surprised.

He said suddenly, confirming my belief, 'You're not taking us to Carnforth House, are you?'

'Not right in,' I said. 'You needn't worry.' I laughed. 'Lemmon just didn't realize how close he was to the hidden treasure, when he knocked me off outside Ottershaw's house.'

'I think the time has come to put me in the picture fully,' Peacock said.

'All in good time. You won't have long to wait now, I promise you.' I told Lemmon to ease down as we came alongside the Ottershaw property, along by the thickly growing trees that fringed the road. We crawled along until we had passed the main gate and were running down the Boroughbridge side. I found the spot where MacDown had pulled the Humber off the road: I believed I could still find my way from there, with the aid of the torches that Peacock had, on my advice, brought with him. 'Here we are,' I said. 'See it, Lemmon? A place to pull off and keep more or less hidden.'

'Okay,' Lemmon said, and stopped. He'd gone a little way past; he backed in neatly, pulling the Jag well clear of the road and facing outwards for a fast getaway afterwards. Peacock asked, 'Did you bury the negatives, or what?'

'Yes,' I told him. 'While MacDown was otherwise engaged, I buried them. They're in a flat cigar tin—small cigars, Picadors.'

He laughed, an excited but nervy sound. 'And X marks the spot!'

'Not quite,' I said, 'but I'll find it, don't you worry about a thing.' I took a last swig at the whisky flask and then we all got out of the car and I led them into the trees. I didn't suppose Peacock was in the least worried just then, but I certainly was. Zero hour was right on top of me now, and in a few moments I would need to do some very fast work indeed. Peacock wouldn't be worried for a very good reason: I wasn't intended to last much longer, though Peacock had gone through a nice little pantomime of stamping the envelope addressed to my bank—first class post, too. Sheer waste of money. He meant to kill me the moment the negatives were unearthed, so it didn't really matter—he would be fifty per cent of infinity better off. Or so he fondly imagined. He was in for a shock, of course, and before it really hit him I had to be on my way out. I said, 'Come on. Follow me.' I was speaking loudly, and unnecessarily since Peacock and the other two were following as closely as they could, but I was feeling a need to keep my courage up and the sound of my own voice helped me to do it. I was moving slowly and with extreme care, for there could be more mantraps around for all I knew. The others were treading equally carefully. What I was aiming for, or rather what I was hoping for without too much confidence, was that Peacock would in fact ram his leg into a trap and then I could make an easy getaway in the confusion. To this end I was trying to pick up the same track, the one that had led me to MacDown that night; but it was almost impossible to be that sure of my surroundings and I knew that if I did happen to lead Peacock or any of them into MacDown's trap it would be the sheerest luck.

After walking through the trees for, I suppose, about ten minutes I had to accept the fact that I was way off the beam this time. I would have to do something fairly fast; Peacock was breathing down my neck now, figuratively and literally, and Lemmon and Phillips were making sounds of weariness that came close to disbelief and mistrust.

I said, since I knew I needed to say something to hold the boat together, 'I think I've missed the path. I'm sorry.'

There was an oath from Lemmon. Peacock hissed, 'Shut up!' I felt his hand on my shoulder, and I stopped. He said, 'I do hope you're not fooling us, Cane. Or trying to, that is. It won't help anybody, least of all you.'

'I'm not trying to fool you,' I said. 'I'll get my bearings in a moment, don't you worry.'

'It was a damfool place to put anything, if you ask me.'

'I don't know about that. You'll agree it was safe. If even I can't find it, who the hell else is going to?'

'Childish reasoning!' he snapped; he was all on edge now and I wasn't surprised. 'People can stumble on things by accident, can't they?'

Yes, sure they can I thought, mantraps; and why the bloody hell don't you! Frankly,

I believed the moment for a breakout had now come. I couldn't keep this charade up successfully for much longer; at the very least, someone's temper was going to crack. It was cold and rather wet and mushy underfoot, and twigs and branches were playing hell with us all and I knew Peacock was losing confidence that I would ever find that cigar tin now. Phillips and Lemmon were starting to grumble really ominously and I had a feeling I was only a couple of jumps ahead of real trouble. So strong was this feeling that I knew I had to take the big risk now and not muck around any longer.

So I stopped, very suddenly, and turned.

Peacock banged into me and I said excitedly, 'It's all right, I've picked it up. It's here.'

'Where?'

'Here,' I said again, and brought my knee up hard in his crutch, with every ounce of my strength behind the blow. As he gave a sharp yell of agony, and doubled, I gave him a smasher to the point of the jaw. He flew back into Lemmon, who, caught right off his guard, went down flat beneath the boss. I lingered just long enough to grab Peacock's gun and then I moved clear. In the light from Peacock's torch, which he had dropped on the ground, I saw Phillips lift his shining cargo-hook and glare round him. He couldn't see me in the surrounding pitch dark, and I wasn't going to fire and give away my position, though I suppose I could in fact have killed him. If he chased me and caught up with me, I would; but just for now it didn't quite constitute self-defence. So instead I slid backwards, quietly, around the trunk of a big tree, and then turned and went on as fast as I could without making too much racket. I heard a lot of confused swearing behind me, but no pursuit. They wouldn't have the least idea which direction I'd gone in, but I expect they were assuming it was towards the Jag and no doubt they would be concentrating on getting there before I did.

I plunged on through the trees and the undergrowth and after a while I found I was climbing a low slope, a kind of mound in the trees. When I reached the top, I saw lights ahead in the near-to-middle distance. I couldn't tell what they were, but it was a fair assumption they were the lighted windows of Carnforth House.

I pressed on. I would probably come to a drive, leading to an exit to the main road. I could hang around, if this should be the case, in cover until Peacock was safely on his way, and then try to thumb a lift to a telephone. I was feeling a surge of excitement now, of real hope at last.

I did come to a drive.

As a matter of fact I came to more than a drive, I came straight to the gravel sweep in front of the house itself. There was a bright light outside the front door, in a stone porticoed porch. The house was Georgian, big and gracious and square. From the porch a dog came padding across the gravel, sniffing the air and making straight for me, on the edge of the trees and no more than ten yards distant.

I kept still and quiet, trying not to waft my scent about.

The dog approached, slowed, stopped, bristled, and barked.

'For God's sake,' I said wearily, 'pack it in, can't you, you smelly little beast?'

The dog was a Pekinese. And it wasn't a bark, it was a horrid yap. It penetrated, evidently, for after half a minute the front door opened and a woman came out. I could see that it was Phyllis Marton. 'Changsi-wangsi,' she called in what I expect she took to be a sugar-sweet tone, 'Changsi-wangsi, darling, what is it, then?'

The yapping proceeded, after one backward glance at Mistress. Changsi-wangsi sat there like God communicating wrathfully with Moses. Mistress came from the porch—foolishly, for anyone could have been lurking in the trees. She didn't come far, though. She spoke to that bloody little Peke again, asking him to tell her what he had found. Not for the first time, I reflected on how insane a woman dog-owner can sound to other ears. I moved, partly I think from sheer irritation, then something sharp penetrated my trousers, entering my backside, and, because for an instant I was convinced it was Phillips's cargo-hook, I gave a short, sharp yelp of pain and surprise, and turned round.

There was nothing there except a lot more prickles: a bloody great blackberry bush. Bravely, Changsi-wangsi charged. Phillis Marton, I saw, was retreating fast to the porch. It was time to come out. I did so, and, fending off the yapping little brute with my foot as best I could, I called out.

'I'm awfully sorry,' I said. 'I can explain everything. The name's Cane.' I was advancing as I spoke, and now I came under the light. I saw relief in her face. I said, 'We met in Drayling, if you remember?'

'Yes,' she said, still rather shaken, 'of course I remember. You wanted to meet Mr Ottershaw...for a job. I'm afraid you haven't chosen a very good time to call.'

'I haven't called about a job,' I said. 'Is Ottershaw in?'

She shook her head. 'No. He's away for a few days, in Newcastle. I'm staying here.' She paused. 'You'll have heard about my husband, I expect.'

'Yes. I'm very sorry.'

'Mr Ottershaw very kindly brought me up to stay with him for a while.'

'Yes,' I said again, 'I gathered that. Mrs Marton, may I come in?'

'Of course you may,' she said. She turned away to the door; I looked at the curious bedfellows made by her unfortunate face and her sensual figure. 'Bedfellows' was just about the word too, in all the circumstances. I followed her into the hall of Ottershaw's house, marvelling at the gall of the man who had invited, to live under his roof, the woman he was using, or had hoped to use until Peacock had butted in, in such a vile way. She couldn't possibly have any idea of the truth. She shut the door behind me and said, 'Just a moment.' She went to a green-baize-covered door at one side of a kind of first-level hall—red-carpeted stairs led up to the main hall—opened it and called down another staircase, 'Mrs Houle? A friend's called—I've let him in. I just thought I'd let you know in case you heard voices.'

'Yes'm,' a voice called back. 'Thank you'm. Will you want me to wait up?'

'No, that's all right, Mrs Houle. Good night.'

'Good night'm.' I looked at my watch: it was just after eleven. I must have been groping around in the trees for a damn sight longer than I'd thought.

Phyllis Marton shut the door to the servants' quarters and led me up into the main hall and then into a long, beautifully-furnished room with three tall windows. She said, 'You don't look very well, Mr Cane. Or Captain Cane, rather—I remember, you see! Would you like some whisky?'

I said, 'I'd love it, but first I'd like a telephone. It's urgent, Mrs Marton, very urgent.'

'There's one in Mr Ottershaw's study. I'm sure he wouldn't mind. I'll show you.'

She did. The study was across the hall and along a passage. She showed me in, flipped the light on, and went out again, leaving me to it. I went over to Ottershaw's desk and sat in a swivel-chair and called Limbrick's home number, the flat off the Edgware Road. Limbrick's woman answered, heard the urgency in my voice, and put Limbrick on pronto. I said, 'It's Cane. Now just listen, will you. MacDown's in trouble, or will be when certain people get busy, and so are my friends the Crimonds.' I passed brief details, and both addresses—I'd noted the number and road of the Kendal house when we were leaving—and asked Limbrick to send the police in strength and bugger keeping matters 'in the family'. He gave me his promise that he would do all he could but didn't commit himself as to the local police.

'Where are you?' he asked.

I said, 'Carnforth House. Mrs Marton's

here—Robert's widow.'

'I knew she was. Question her, Cane. Press her. You've got a good opportunity now. And don't worry about the rest.'

He rang off. Slowly, I put the handset down. It was perhaps a little extreme, a little exaggerated, to say that Peacock had aroused doubts in my mind about Limbrick as a result of his wild theorising; but I did hope Limbrick was on the level!

I went back to the drawing-room. Phyllis Marton was standing in front of the empty grate, with her hands behind her back, and legs apart, like a man warming his bottom. She was wearing a very plain red dress that showed off her figure to the fullest advantage; if you didn't look at her face, she was ravishing. The whisky was on a tray, a silver tray; there was a cut-glass decanter, a siphon and two glasses.

'Did you get through all right?' she asked perfunctorily.

'Yes, thank you.'

She smiled, and indicated the whisky. 'Would you like to pour, Captain Cane?'

'Thank you.' I went towards the tray; there was a curious atmosphere in that drawing-room, something I didn't quite understand—didn't understand at all as it turned out. 'How d'you like yours?' I asked.

'Three fingers, straight.'

I looked up in surpise. 'Straight? Not just a splash?'

'No. Straight. Absolutely straight.'

I shrugged. It was like a man again, and not many men at that, really. Maybe it went with the rugged face, and the jaw, I don't know. I poured. As a matter of fact, I didn't squirt much soda into mine. Despite Peacock's flask I felt in need of something pretty stiff, especially in view of Limbrick's order to question Phyllis Marton here and now. I hadn't been ready for that, though I suppose I should have been. I was doing a job, after all. But I wasn't very experienced yet and it had seemed to me that for the time being my job was over once I'd done what I could do to ensure safety for MacDown and Bill and Eve Crimond.

I handed Phyllis Marton her glass and she said, 'Thank you, Captain Cane.' She gave her shoulders a curious sort of twist and lift, flattening what there was of her stomach. It was quite a sexy movement, and I could see the nipples straining sharply at the thin material of the dress. Then she drank off the whisky in three quick gulps and turned to set the empty glass on the chimneypiece behind her. She stood there watching me and I found I was mentally undressing her, seeing that body in the positions as shown in the photographs. If only she knew what I'd seen, I thought, she wouldn't be standing there quite so bloody calmly!

You never can tell with women, though. Her next words took my breath away. She said, 'Well, get on with the questions, then, Captain Cane.'

I gaped; she laughed, a brittle sound. When I could speak I asked, 'What questions?'

'The ones your Mr Limbrick told you to ask.'

I was still flabbergasted but this time I ticked over. 'You have an extension phone?'

'In a house this size? Of course there's one. Didn't you hear the click, Captain Cane?'

I said, 'If I did, I wasn't conscious of thinking about it. I...well, I wouldn't have been expecting that. It's a pretty dirty trick, isn't it, listening to other people's conversations?'

She laughed again. 'Poor Captain Cane!

You're not in the service now, you know, you've left chivalry and doing the decent thing and thinking of the honour of the regiment, behind you, Captain Cane. You're in a hard, hard world now. You'll learn—especially in the job you've landed for yourself!'

'How did you know about that?' I asked.

She said, 'I didn't, until I listened in. Oh, you can think it's a dirty trick if you like, but after all, it does concern me, doesn't it?' She turned and took up her glass and left the fireplace and went across to the decanter and poured herself another scotch, as big as the last one and as straight. She drank it. She held the empty glass against her chest, between her breasts, and looked away over my head with an absent sort of look, a look into far distances. Then she said, 'Before the interrogation starts, Captain Cane. I have something I'd like to show you. I won't be a moment.'

She walked out of the room, leaving me alone. I got up and wandered around, restlessly, looking at the furniture and the oil paintings on the walls. She was gone about five minutes, I think, and when she came back she was wearing a short dressing-gown of vivid scarlet, and her feet and legs were bare. She walked to the fireplace and turned, and let the dressing-gown slide to her ankles and stood before me completely naked.

CHAPTER EIGHT

The breasts were large but firm, and the nipples were erect in their brown-coloured circles. She had a narrow waist, a flat stomach in which the navel stood like a questioning eye above that part that sloped away between the thighs. She moved her buttocks seductively, and lifted her arms above her head, and smiled down at me. Her skin was a dark cream, smooth and just faintly tanned all over. To run one's eye upwards to the face was a shock. Then, and only then, Phyllis Marton became an apology for a woman.

I licked my lips; they felt very dry. 'What's the idea?' I asked. 'Are you telling me, in effect, that you knew about those photographs?'

Still with her arms raised, she nodded. 'I knew,' she said.

'And your husband?'

'Yes.'

'He knew too?'

'Yes. They were taken at Drayling. Not by Robert, I might add.'

'But why?'

She laughed. 'I think you're a little naïve, Captain Cane, aren't you?'

I said, 'Money means that much to you, does it?'

'It wasn't only money. There was...an extra thrill in it—in being photographed. In being *watched*.'

I asked, 'Did Marton know—Harold Marton, I mean, your brother-in-law?'

'Of course not,' she said, laughing again. 'That was the whole point, wasn't it?'

'The blackmail?'

'Yes.'

'You were willing to do that to him—your husband was willing to do that to his own brother?'

She said in an absolutely matter-of-fact voice, 'Drayling was terribly expensive to keep up, fantastically expensive, and Robert couldn't bear any thought of parting with it. That would really have been the end.

Harold wouldn't have wanted him to, either. *Family* reasons, you see. Besides, Robert hated having to take in paying guests. It grated terribly. All that would have stopped, you see. He knew he couldn't help making a lot of money, this way.'

'Where did Ottershaw come in?' I wanted to check her version against Peacock's. As it happened, the two versions tallied. Ottershaw, she said, had been sent the negatives.

I asked, who by?

She said, 'My husband, of course. Anonymously. The reason for sending them being that he preferred not to be personally involved in direct blackmail. And he knew Ottershaw would jump at it—he knew how that man's mind worked, what a fixation he had about government expenditure and taxes and all that—'

'Then the night he was killed—your husband, I mean—he was going to the vault to get the rest of the set?'

'How d'you mean?' she asked. She was puzzled now. She had dropped her arms, and had folded them across her breasts, and was standing with the mound of Venus thrust seductively forward. 'Why should he go to the vault for them, if

185

by vault you mean the family place in the churchyard?'

'That's what I mean,' I confirmed. 'It so happens that I know there was a set there, and it was the set your husband sent to Ottershaw. You must have known Ottershaw lost them after they were handed over? That they were stolen from him?'

She said, 'No, I didn't know that,' and suddenly she looked scared. 'You said *the rest* of the set. Was that significant?'

'Well, I'd doubt if he'd have parted with the whole lot to Ottershaw.'

She said, 'But he did. You see, he could always get more, couldn't he?'

I suppose I *was* naïve. 'Yes,' I said, 'I'd forgotten that. He had the gang-bang show right on the premises, hadn't he! Now, would you like to know who it was that pinched those negatives from Ottershaw, Mrs Marton?'

She nodded.

I told her, and asked if she knew Peacock, or Lemmon or the others. I wasn't surprised when she said she had never heard of them, and I believed her. I said, 'Well, they've lost them again, but they're after them and they may find them. How would you feel about being exposed

186

literally and negatively if you follow—if you don't make any cash out of it for yourself, Mrs Marton?'

She said, 'Well, obviously, not so good as if I had.' She laughed.

'You've no actual shame about it?'

'None at all. Why should I have? Why should I be ashamed of my body, Captain Cane?'

'The photographs,' I said, 'were fairly extreme posture-wise. Don't you remember?'

She nodded. 'Yes,' she said, 'of course I remember. All that was natural too, between a man and a woman.'

'Sure,' I agreed. 'In private. But I suppose that's not the point now. What really matters is, are you going to help me get my hands on the negatives before they lead to any more trouble?'

'How can I help?'

I said, 'For a start, you can give me some idea who might have got hold of them. There couldn't have been all that many people in the know, surely. Ottershaw, your husband, the man who took them, and Peacock's boyos. It seems to me it could all narrow down to the photographer. Who was he, Mrs Marton?'

'None of your business,' she said. 'Anyway, it wouldn't be him, would it?'

'Why not?'

'As the photographer, he'd hardly need to do any stealing. If he'd had that in mind, all he had to do was take a few more while he was about it.'

'That's a point, but it doesn't necessarily follow. He could simply have wanted Peacock *not* to have access to them. But why not tell me who he was?'

She said obstinately, 'I'm just not going to, that's all. I mean that, Captain Cane.'

'All right,' I said, shrugging. I supposed there was a chance she didn't even know. Her husband might have fixed all that. 'Tell me something else, then: why the current nudity?'

I was watching her face, because it acted as a kind of repellant and I needed to keep a level head. I saw the slow smile that spread across the coarse, ugly features, saw the lips move apart and the end of the tongue flick through momentarily. She said, 'You don't know? You really don't know?'

She came towards me then and from the way she moved I knew, if I hadn't known before, that she was hopelessly nympho. Absolutely no man would be safe with Phyllis Marton, and because her keen financial instinct ensured that she combined business with pleasure, the photographer might already be aiming his lens from some hiding place. I don't deny the temptation as that perfect body loomed over me. I looked with fascination at the contours, the curves, the folds, the light-brown tiny curls of hair, the smooth creaminess of her skin. She was big and strong and obviously immensely capable, and her desire could almost be felt as something tangible descending upon me. I felt her hands on my clothing, moving around my waist and then downwards. Temptation slid towards surrender. I felt her breath, warm on my cheeks now, and even that smelled of some intense bodily desire, some chemistry of sex. I felt that it was all totally inevitable now, that I would be quite unable to resist. Let the photographic evidence be produced in the morning, let her make her financial demands after her sexual ones, let her threaten me with Limbrick, I didn't care! Whatever else she was, and however grim her face, she was still a woman who knew how to use her body.

Later, when we had slept a little, I stirred and said, 'Now let's have the reckoning, shall we?'

She lifted herself on one elbow, and looked down at me. In the dim light, the heavy face looked almost womanly, as though what we had been doing had brought her femininity to the surface for a while. She asked, 'What do you mean by that, John?'

I said, 'Why the photographs, of course.'

She laughed, a lazy and contented sound. 'There haven't been any this time.'

'You surprise me!'

'For one thing, there's only Mrs Houle in the house—Ottershaw's housekeeper.'

'And she doesn't take photographs?'

She laughed again. 'Not this sort.'

I said, 'I wish you'd tell me who does. Who did, I mean.'

'No.'

'But why not?'

She said, 'Because if you knew that, you'd have your proof, wouldn't you?'

'And I haven't already, after what you told me earlier?'

'No! Think about it, John. What does it consist of?'

190

I said, 'Plenty.'

'Oh no, it doesn't! There's nothing beyond what you knew already, basically.'

'Except that you have incriminated yourself.'

'Oh, no, I haven't! Not as regards blackmail. I've only incriminated Robert, and he's dead. Besides which, I'd stopped loving him,' she added as if it excused everything.

'You're a bitch,' I said.

She shrugged. 'Sticks and stones may break my bones.'

'That's the sort of thing MacDown would say.' I thought about MacDown; I hoped the police had got to him before Peacock got the Jag home to Kendal. But then Peacock, unless he were a fool, would be avoiding Kendal. I was suddenly conscious of the fact that I was wasting a hell of a lot of time, though in a sense it could all be put down to following out Limbrick's instruction to question Phyllis Marton. In any case, I hadn't any idea what to do next, except perhaps to get hold of a car, or a train, and go south to Drayling. There just might be some clues around the Marton vault, which indeed represented the sum total of my recovery knowledge to date—the information from Peacock that the negatives had once been there. And I was beginning to form the impression that the man who had removed them *must* have been the man who had done the photography. It was unlikely that anyone else would have been in the know.

I sat up. 'What's the time?' I asked, and looked at my own watch. 0200 hours exactly. I had been here about three hours; it was time I moved out, only there wouldn't be any transport around. I asked Phyllis Marton if she felt like driving me into York.

'What's the point?' she asked.

'There'll be a train coming through from the north during the night.'

'Where d'you want to go?'

'London,' I lied.

'To see this Limbrick?'

'Correct.'

'And tell him what? That I'm a bitch, which is about all you've discovered, Captain Cane?'

She mocked me. I really didn't care; I was too damn tired. She said, 'Anyway, the answer's no. I haven't a car as it happens. Ottershaw drove me up, and he's taken his with him.'

'What about his wife?'

'She's touring the Continent with hers.'

'Oh. So I stay here till I can ring for a hire car from Boroughbridge, is that it?'

She grinned; her face still held that womanly look. 'Do you mind?'

I said, 'No, not all that much.' After all, I was a bachelor and even in this permissive age bachelors don't get the chance every night. Her arms went round me again and I had a few guilty thoughts about the Crimonds, and MacDown, and Limbrick, and then I let them all go right out of my mind. I'd done what I could.

I've no idea what Mrs Houle could possibly have thought, unless she was used to her employer carrying on in his wife's absence and was well paid to keep her trap shut. She didn't look the sort for that, though. She was old-fashioned country-servant material, used to good service and gentlemen's houses, and though I dare say Ottershaw was quite a come-down she would have maintained her own standards. Any funny business and her notice would have gone in like a shot from a gun, probably—and, after last night, probably would. Not that she found Phyllis Marton naked. My large and rumbustious light o'love had gone upstairs to dress just as dawn woke the birds in the trees and when Mrs Houle came in to flick a duster round before getting breakfast she found us there talking respectably as if we'd been at it all night. Talking, I mean. It looked very innocent, but I don't suppose Mrs Houle was fooled for a moment.

Frigidly she said, 'I didn't know the gentleman was staying. I didn't really'm.'

'We found so much to talk about, Mrs Houle,' Phyllis Marton said without a blush or a flicker. 'The time really flew past. I expect the Captain could do with some breakfast, if you'd be so good, Mrs Houle.'

'Yes, well. Yes'm, all right.' Mrs Houle marched to the door; there was a certain amount of dudgeon. Phyllis Marton called her back. 'Yes'm?' she said from the door.

'Captain Cane is in a hurry to get back to London. I wonder, would you mind telephoning for a car to come out here at...let's say, eight o'clock sharp?'

'Yes'm.'

'Thank you, Mrs Houle,' I said. When she had gone I stood up and looked down on Phyllis Marton. 'I suppose you realize,'

I said, 'that you're in dead trouble from now on out?'

She was calm enough about that. 'Although I didn't know it, I suppose I have been ever since those negatives first got into the wrong hands, haven't I? Nothing's changed at all.'

'I'm not referring to the authorities.'

'Neither am I,' she said, smiling. 'They wouldn't dare lift a finger, openly I mean, because of Harold. I know you've been sent to put the stopper on the blackmail, if ever you can make anything stick to anyone, but as you very well know it would all have been done with the utmost discretion. Wouldn't it?'

I said, 'I don't know, I can't answer for Limbrick or his bosses. But just listen to me for a moment. You could be in danger, you know. There's not much chivalry wrapped up in all this.'

'You mean Peacock, and Lemmon, and Clapp, the ones you asked if I knew?'

'And Phillips. You'll have to watch it. I'd say you'd have a little difficulty in explaining to the police, if you were thinking of asking for protection.'

'Oh, but I wasn't thinking of that at all. Really.'

'What then? You're just going to risk it?'

She looked at me. Dressed, she was hideous again, though not quite as unattractive as before since now I had seen her with a closer eye than the camera. 'Do you think I ought to?' she asked.

I said, 'That's entirely up to you.'

'You mean its not your job to advise?'

'That's right. I'm sorry. All I have to do is get the negatives back, and if you can't help, or won't help—'

'All right,' she broke in. 'I understand. But you can always advise me as a man, can't you? Unofficially?'

I said, 'Yes, I suppose so.'

'Well?'

Feeling suddenly irritated by her persistence I snapped, 'You'd be a damn fool to take any risks where Peacock and the others are concerned. Frankly, we're lucky they didn't turn up here during the night.' I said that mainly to scare her; though I'd had the thought at the back of my mind, I hadn't really considered Peacock likely to linger in the vicinity once he'd lost me—he would have plenty of things to see to elsewhere. I went on, 'I'd have thought you'd have realized the dangers for yourself, seeing how much money's potentially involved in all this.'

'Perhaps I did,' she said, and smiled. 'Perhaps I did, but now that you've actually said it yourself, I don't see how you can—well, disagree with what I'm going to do.'

I gave her a sharp look. 'And that is?'

'I'm coming to London with you,' she said crisply. 'But before you start to develop any ideas of your own, let me tell you this; I'm *not* going to see your Mr Limbrick. I've nothing to tell him that I haven't already told you, anyway.'

I believed her; if I hadn't, I suppose I could have arrested her; though nobody had ever been precise about my powers in that direction, I did rank as a kind of makeshift copper. I decided I had better let her do as she wished—she would certainly be safer and I didn't much want Peacock's mob to get their hands on her—but the trouble was, I hadn't really intended going as far as London. Still, it wasn't all that far back to Drayling and I could pick up my own car while I was in London.

So I said, 'All right, come along if you like. What about Ottershaw?'

'What about him?'

'Are you going to let him know?'

She smiled. 'It's only polite, isn't it? I'll ring him from London.'

'What'll you say?'

'You mean you don't want me to say anything about you and the negatives?'

I said, 'Not only do I not want you to say a word about any of that, but I'll have to insist that you don't.'

Again she smiled. 'Official Secrets Act?'

'Something like that.'

'I'll be very, very discreet and careful,' she promised. 'I'll tell him I felt restless, all alone up here. It'll sound quite natural. I wanted to get to town and talk to people I knew. I've a female cousin in Knightsbridge, and I shall stay with her, if you think that's all right?'

'It's perfectly all right,' I said. Of course there was still Mrs Houle who would no doubt report everything, but that was a chance I'd have had to take whether or not Phyllis Marton came with me. To attempt to put some innocent sounding but phony explanation across to Mrs Houle would only make things much worse...

Soon after this, Mrs Houle came in with breakfast. Fried eggs and bacon, toast and marmalade, and coffee. It was just what I needed, and it did me a lot of good, especially the coffee and the cigarette that went with it. After breakfast Phyllis told Mrs Houle she was leaving for London with me. I saw the look in the housekeeper's eye, and the way her back stiffened. But I could also see her thinking it was none of her responsibility, Mrs Marton was not part of her household, and if she wanted to go it was her own affair and good riddance.

'Yes'm,' was all she said, and then she left the room, head high and a hairpin drooping from the old-fashioned, tight bun at the back of her neck.

At 0800 hours, when the hired car came up the drive right on the dot, Phyllis Marton was ready with two cases packed. Mrs Houle saw us off. The car took us into York, and the railway station. I bought two tickets to Kings Cross, and then we had time to kill. We walked around and looked at the Minster and the restoration work, and we climbed to the old city wall and walked a little way along that too. I was all eyes that morning, watching out for Peacock's mob and for Ottershaw as well, though he could hardly have made it from Newcastle just yet even if Mrs Houle had been on the blower before we were down the drive. I was also to some extent preoccupied with my thoughts and was wondering if I should ring Limbrick, or the local police, for news of the Crimonds and Chief Superintendent MacDown. But I decided not to. It wouldn't serve any useful purpose other than to set my own mind at rest and so far as that was concerned it wouldn't be long now before I talked to Limbrick in person.

We saw no Peacocks and no Ottershaws in York, and when the London express drew us out of York station for the south, the run was equally uneventful. At Kings Cross I grabbed a taxi and delivered Phyllis Marton at her cousin's address in Knightsbridge, took a note of her phone number and gave her that of my digs, and then I went on to the Edgware Road and Limbrick. I hadn't warned him I was coming, but he was in as it happened, and he was surprised to see me.

'You get around, Cane,' he said. 'How's Yorkshire?'

'Dangerous,' I said. 'How's MacDown?'

'Safe. So are your friends the Crimonds.'

I let out a long breath. I was very relieved, about MacDown no less than

Bill and Eve. I quite liked the old chap. 'Where is MacDown?' I asked.

Limbrick pushed a silver box of cigarettes across, taking one himself. 'Still in Kendal, at the nick. Feels he could be useful up there.' He gave me a sharpish look; maybe I should have felt the same. 'You'll want to know what happened after you rang from Carnforth House.'

'Yes.'

'The police went in, in strength. Drayling and Kendal. Nothing happened in Drayling. In Kendal, they made it before Peacock and the others got back there, and they found MacDown and Clapp. They waited.'

'In hiding? An ambush?'

Limbrick nodded. 'Correct.'

'So they're all in the bag?'

'No! They never did come back. They scarpered *en route*. They got clean away, what's more. So far, there's no trace.'

I groaned, though of course I'd expected this. 'Back to square one. I haven't got all that far myself. Still, there's Clapp. Where's he now?'

'In the nick at Kendal, being questioned by MacDown in person. The last report indicated no progress at all. Clapp's not talking. He's got his solicitor there and he's still not talking. MacDown, however, is a patient man, very patient. Now let's have your story, Cane, in full detail, please.'

I gave it to him. He listened closely, without interrupting. He asked his questions at the end. He was interested in Phyllis Marton. 'Any ideas as to why she won't give the name of the photographer?' he asked.

'Not really,' I said. 'She may not know it, though that wasn't what she said.'

'Then I'd say she does know it. From all I hear, she doesn't sound the sort of woman to...well, tease. Don't bother to make a funny joke about that, Cane. You know what I mean. She wouldn't pretend to knowledge she hadn't got just to make some kind of impression. To recap, now; she simply told you she wouldn't give you his name?'

'That's right,' I said.

Limbrick frowned. 'Shielding him, of course. Why? Is the reason a financial one?'

I shrugged. 'I don't know. I suppose it must be. What else is there?'

Limbrick said, 'Love.'

'*Love?* Phyllis Marton?' I laughed, hollowly.

Limbrick said, 'I say again—love. Don't laugh. She's a woman, isn't she?'

'Yes,' I said, 'and she loves sex, all right! But a man, no. Not as such.'

'I wouldn't be too sure of that,' Limbrick said quietly. 'I really wouldn't. *Cherchez l'homme,* I rather think. But of course, even if we find the photographer, we don't necessarily find the negatives. In fact, there's probably no connexion between the photographer and the present whereabouts of the results of his labours.'

'That's what I said—back to square one.'

'Oh, I don't know about that,' Limbrick said mildly. 'As—'

'Time,' I butted in, 'is almost up. Isn't it?'

'Not quite. We've won an extension. The debate's been put forward twenty-four hours. The opposition's hopping mad, and look like making themselves awkward, but that gives us till the day after tomorrow.'

'Three cheers for that,' I said. 'How's the Prime Minister feeling now?'

'Bloody frightened,' Limbrick said. 'D'you know something, Cane?'

'What?'

'If I had those negatives in my hands right now, why, I'd virtually be the ruler of Britain. I could ask for, and get, literally anything I liked! Civil List pension of a hundred thousand quid a year, a peerage—dukedom even—permission to park my car outside my own bloody house, if I had a house fronting on the street. With full authority to make rude signs at all traffic wardens.' He grinned. 'But you and I both know what I *will* get, Cane.'

'Go on,' I said.

'Officially, a thank-you and a good mark in my copybook. Unofficially, the enmity of the Prime Minister. He'll avoid my eye at official functions and he may even find an excuse to pension me off into early retirement. Four hundred years ago, he'd have had my head cut off. And if you're not a bloody fool, Cane, you know why.'

Slowly, I nodded. 'Yes. You've seen him as a scared little man. You've seen him, I imagine, more or less grovelling. He won't forgive you for that. Life's unfair at times, isn't it?'

'You can say that again,' Limbrick said savagely.

'I'll say something else,' I said. 'Something I should have told you before, but didn't.'

'Well?'

'I told you Peacock suggested I was Ottershaw's man. But I didn't tell you he also suggested I was in cahoots with *you.*'

Limbrick said, 'I trust you are, Cane. I trust you are.'

'Sure. But what he meant was, we were both bent. We were going to really clean up over this.'

'I see. And you?'

I said, 'Well, I'm being honest in telling you.'

'That doesn't quite answer my question, does it?'

'*I* don't think you're bent,' I said. 'I've done a lot of thinking around the point, though, and I may as well admit it. I didn't know you from Adam when we met in Trader Vic's. It was all a little chancey, one way and another. Come to that, I still don't know you. That house—that interview board that was convened. The chaps that were there, and the girl. They could all have been fixed, couldn't they? It could all have been set up. When a thing's as hush as your job, well, outsiders are easily fooled—you know what I mean. There's just one thing that stands out a mile as dead honest.'

'I'm so glad. And what's that, Cane?'

I grinned. 'A rock of virtue and probity, and its name's MacDown. You could never have fooled that man in a million years.'

'I'm delighted,' Limbrick said icily, 'to have your accolade. I suppose you realize you've been damned impertinent and rude, as well as bloody silly?'

'I'm sorry,' I said. 'It was just that...well, when you spoke of what you *could* get out of this job if it's successful, and contrasted it with what you *would* get out of it...I was reminded of what Peacock said. That's all. I never said I believed it. In fact I said the opposite, if you remember.'

'Yes,' Limbrick said. He was white with anger. 'Well, of course, you were right to tell me. Perhaps I should also tell you that I'm thanking God you're only in the department on a temporary basis.'

'My prayers go right up alongside yours, all the way,' I said. 'You can fire me whenever you want, Limbrick. I don't like stinking disused wells in the Yorkshire

Dales, or dirty beds in Kendal, or men like Lemmon and Clapp and so on. Or the possible involvement of my friends, people like Bill and Eve Crimond.'

Limbrick shrugged. 'You know the alternative. Still, that's your affair. In the meantime, you're still working for me. Want to be a mutineer?'

I sighed. 'No. Having got this far, I'll see it through.'

'I see. Frankly, I'm not sure that I really want you to—oh, it's nothing to do with what you've just said. Thing is, it may be getting beyond you, Cane.'

I said something rude to that.

'You've not yet reached professional status,' he reminded me. 'Far from it! I recruited you largely because of Drayling. Now this has moved way beyond Drayling, you could get out of your depth, and this thing's vital. On the other hand...' he shrugged.

'On the other hand,' I said, 'it may *not* have moved beyond Drayling. Also I know the background now, and the characters involved, don't I?'

'That's just what I was about to say. It'd take too damn long now, to get someone else into the picture—and into the feel of it. So I'll have to settle for you, won't I?'

'Careful of the flattery,' I said with heavy sarcasm. 'It might go to my head. I don't really want to go on with this in the very least—except that I hate leaving a job half finished.'

'You did that with the army,' Limbrick said.

'I know—I've realized that since. That's why I don't want to do it again.' There was a short silence after that, and I broke it by saying, 'Well, what's next, then? Or do we just sit around and see what MacDown achieves with Clapp?'

Limbrick was about to answer when his telephone rang. Still looking angry, he answered it. He didn't say much, he just grunted, mostly; but he scribbled on a jotter beside the phone. When he rang off he looked at me and said, 'Funny you should have mentioned MacDown. That was him on the line. Clapp's talked. Just a little. It could be enough. That I want you to find out. Will you?'

'I've already said, I'll finish the job.'

'Good man. Get across to Soho. Twenty-three Dalzeil Street. It's a pornographic bookshop and it's run by a Greek called

Kontannis. Photography also takes place there. Put the screw on Kontannis, Cane, and look after yourself while you're doing it. All right?'

'Just a minute,' I said. 'What exactly did Clapp say?'

'That a man who works for Kontannis could have been the photographer in this case. I gather Peacock didn't know this, so it looks as if Clapp was also in business on his own account—as a double-crosser. This may not help—we're agreed that the man who took the shots probably isn't the one who nicked the negatives from that vault in Drayling, but it's all we have.'

'All right,' I said. I got to my feet. 'I suppose MacDown didn't give the name of this man?'

'Yes.' Limbrick glanced at his jotter pad. 'The name's Ivery, with an e.' He looked at me in some surprise after he'd said that, because I had reacted much more than he had expected. 'What's the matter, Cane?'

I said, 'A certain amount of shock, that's all. Events close in upon us again! Ivery's the name of the female cousin Phyllis Marton is staying with in Knightsbridge.'

CHAPTER NINE

Clapp, I reflected as I headed for Soho, had probably been getting out from under: the first rat to leave what he may have begun to see as a sinking ship. I hadn't yet seen MacDown in action as an interrogator, but I could well imagine he was persistent, and wily too. Clapp was laying up treasure in heaven, as it were, rather than in Kendal or wherever it was he would have flown to once the wealth from the blackmail had started rolling.

But where did Phyllis Marton fit now?

A moment's further thought told me there wasn't any basic shift in her position, however. As I had told Limbrick, she had never denied *knowing* the photographer's identity, and I suppose her cousin's husband—as I assumed this Ivery to be—was as good as anyone else. It kept it all in the family, too.

I found Dalzeil Street, one of the maze of smelly little alley-like byways lying between Berwick Street and the Charing

Cross Road. Number 23 was just like any of the other pornographic bookshops that proliferate in Soho. Its window was a feast of literature dealing with whips and other sadistic erotica, with positioning and perversion and all that. There was nothing explicitly to suggest photography, but to the enquiring mind this would hardly be necessary. I hadn't come down with the last shower myself, but, just in case I had, I suppose, Limbrick had filled me in on some of the detail.

'I don't know this outfit personally,' he'd said, 'but the form's much the same throughout the business. A good deal of their trade will be done in obscene photography—it's very profitable, and they pay well for subjects. they can afford to, and there's a constant demand for the raw material. Any man or woman with a sexy body can expect to earn up to a hundred quid for an hour's posing with a partner.'

'Each?'

'Each. It's money easily earned, and I dare say not unpleasurably.' Limbrick grinned. 'You're well-built, Cane. It could always be worth bearing in mind, after you leave us.'

'Very funny,' I said. 'Where's the market for this finished product? America?'

'No, they have plenty of the domestic supply over there. It's mostly for home consumption. It goes out through advertisements in the shadier magazines, or even from under the counter of the bookshop itself. There's also a steady trade with prostitutes, who use the photographs to help stimulate their customers' appetites— and, in their turn, sometimes sell them at a nice profit afterwards. I suggest you put yourself in the second category, Cane.'

'What d'you mean?'

'Be a direct bookshop customer. Ask to see the stock.'

'You don't think the time has come for more basic methods? For a straightforward approach, a demand to see this Ivery?'

'No. If I thought that, I'd be inclined to hand over to the ordinary Force. But I don't. This whole thing still needs discreet handling. Besides, it'll be good experience for you!'

'I thought I was going to get the sack?'

'I keep an open mind,' Limbrick said.

I remembered his words while I studied the contents of the window at 23 Dalzeil Street. Not the words about the sack, or about what I could choose as a career thereafter, but what he had said about the continuing need for discretion. He was an experienced man, was Limbrick. I certainly was not. But I felt pretty strongly that he was making a mistake, all the same. We had Clapp's word now, extracted by MacDown, the word that would incriminate photograper Ivery. In my view, Ivery should be brought in pronto and put under the official grill, and broken right open. Whatever we had thought, or rather whatever I had thought, in the past about who had the missing negatives, Ivery *could* know where they were. In fact this shop could be a very safe place to hide them away in; they could mingle unobtrusively with the stock! Hard pressure applied to Ivery could yield them up faster than I could hope to winnow them out by the careful use of discretion. And I thought speed was important.

Limbrick, however, was the boss.

I pushed the door open and went in. There was a youngish man, behind a book-piled counter, a man bald before his time, with a pale and puffy face reddened by an incipient boil beside the nose. He wore a mauve blouse—at least, blouse is the nearest I can get to identification of the garment. He said, 'Good afternoon, can I help you?'

I felt furtive anyway, so it wasn't hard to look it. I cast a glance over my shoulder, then bent towards the man. I said, 'I was wondering if you had any photographs—you know what I mean?'

He looked blank; this was part of the formalities, I assumed. You didn't just flog pornography like saucy postcards at the seaside. He said, 'Well, I don't know if I do, do I?'

'Nudes,' I said.

'Stimulants,' he said.

'That's right,' I said.

He lifted a flap in the counter. 'Come inside,' he invited. I did. I walked ahead of him into a dimly lit back room, its walls filled with shelves of books. There was another door giving on to the rear of the premises. He said, 'Okay, now you can talk.'

I felt helpless, out of my depth. I asked, 'What have you got?'

He shrugged. 'I haven't said I've got anything, mate. I'm waiting for you. First: who sent you?'

The penny dropped. This man didn't

open up till he was dead sure he wasn't being called on by the cops. A wise precaution, no doubt. I had to think very fast indeed, and I said, 'Just a friend. A friend who also knows Mr Kontannis. I'd rather like a word with Mr Kontannis himself, as a matter of fact—'

'I am Mr Kontannis.'

I was surprised. 'You've no accent,' I said.

'I've never been to Greece. I was born here in Soho. Who was this friend, this mutual friend?'

Once again I felt out of my depth. I thought, bugger Limbrick! He talked about discretion and the indirect approach, yet he'd also told me, quite plainly, to put the screw on Kontannis. Faced with what seemed to be a choice, I indulged my nature and took the latter course. Risking it being construed as blatant disobedience later, I said, 'Ivery. He works for you, doesn't he, Mr Kontannis?'

'If you say so.'

'That's my information. Doesn't he?'

Mr Kontannis shook his head. 'He used to. Not any more. He walked out three days ago.'

That rocked me, but I felt I was getting

warmer. 'Why did he do that?' I asked.

'Said he wanted a change. He didn't tell you?'

'No.'

'Yet he's a friend?'

'An acquaintance. I haven't seen him for some time, in point of fact.'

Kontannis looked at me hard; the pale face was starting to shine with a film of sweat, but that could have been just the heat of the room. It was horribly close. He asked, 'Who are you? What's your name? What do you want? You don't just want to buy photographs.'

'No,' I said, 'that's true, I don't. Not just *any* photographs, that is. I'm not going to tell you who I am, Mr Kontannis. But I'll tell you what I want, and it's this: I want to talk about Ivery. For instance, do you happen to know if he ever did any free-lancing?'

'I wouldn't know if he did. It would have been up to him, no business of mine, so long as he didn't steal my customers. Why do you ask?

I grinned. 'That's *my* business, Mr Kontannis. Where's Ivery now?'

'I told you, he left.'

'Yes. I mean, what's his address?'

Kontannis shook his head. 'I don't know.'

'An employee, and you didn't know where he lived?'

'I mean he has gone from that address.'

'Oh. You checked?'

'Yes.'

'Why?'

'To deliver his insurance card.'

I nodded; that could have been true, of course. I said, 'He's just vanished, without trace?'

'Seems like it, yes. I don't know any more than I've told you. I don't know who you are, but you talk like you was a copper. You've nothing on me, mate.'

'Oh, not much!' I said sardonically. 'If I was a copper, and checked through your real stock, Kontannis, I reckon I could have you so fast your feet just wouldn't touch the ground on the way to the nick!'

'So you're not a copper?' There was disbelief in the tone when he asked that.

I smiled. 'Like the Prime Minister, Kontannis, I can neither confirm nor deny such a rumour. Get me?'

He stared at me, and licked his lips. I saw fear in the eyes now. I smiled again and shifted myself towards an untidy desk in a corner of the room, a desk with a telephone on it. I rested my rump on the desk-top, close to the telephone. I said, 'Yes, Kontannis. The Prime Minister...a man of many worries. You wouldn't really want to add to them, I'm sure—not just for Ivery's benefit. What was the split going to be, Kontannis?'

He licked again at his lips. 'I don't know what you're talking about,' he said, his voice shaking.

'It's too late for that,' I said. 'Clapp has blown the lot.' It was an exaggeration, but that didn't matter. I reached out for the telephone with my left hand and used my right to inhibit Mr Kontannis as he advanced. 'I'm going to go through your stock, my friend, and you're not going to interfere. But I'm going to need a little assistance.' I dialled Limbrick's number. I don't really know what I would have said to him and for all I knew he might have gone hopping mad at an indiscretion, but as it happened I didn't get him. I had only dialled the first three numbers when the other door came open, the one leading into the back premises, and I saw a three parts-naked girl. I doubt if she was more than eighteen and she had very striking breasts. Her hand flew to her mouth on seeing me, and she gasped, and Mr Kontannis took full advantage of my temporary distraction. He reached behind him with a lightning movement and then something very hard and heavy took me on the side of my head and that, for a while was all I knew.

When I came round I couldn't at first place my surroundings. There was movement somewhere beneath me, and a loud rattle, and the sound of an engine, and a good deal of swaying. It was dark and someone was flashing a torch now and again. It took me quite a while to realize that I was in the back of a closed van, going somewhere fast. I was on the floor and I was tied up, wrists and ankles like in that well up by Semerwater, and I was accompanied, the torch told me, by Lemmon; and God alone knew where he had materialized from. When I felt capable I asked him, but he wouldn't say. I lost interest anyhow when I became increasingly aware of something alongside me, something close, that kept kind of flopping closer each time the van lurched to the left. It was cold and flabby and lifeless. It was in fact a dead body. I had to suffer it, because I was already hard against the van's side and was helpless. I could see in the back-glow from the torch that Lemmon was watching the expression on my face. He was grinning away pleasurably, too. I asked whose the body was.

'Don't say you don't know,' he answered in mock amazement. 'Well, well.'

The well, well brought back nasty memories. I said, 'Of course I don't know.'

'It's your old pal.'

'Which old pal?' I thought, with horror, of MacDown. I tried to see the face, but couldn't. 'Come on, Lemmon!'

He said, 'The one you *said* was your old pal. You told Kontannis. Ivery!'

'Oh,' I said. Things clicked into place. 'So that was where he went...and that's why he'd left Kontannis's employment, I suppose!'

'Correct,' Lemmon said. 'He took the photos, Ivery did—Kontannis said you knew that. And by that I mean, he nicked the negatives. Which you *didn't* know.' He was hugely pleased with himself. 'Call it a verbal misunderstanding.'

My head swam. This was getting way

beyond me. 'You mean he wasn't the photographer at all?'

'Also correct,' Lemmon said. 'He was just the thief. Dirty bastard. We got it out of Kontannis. Kontannis and Ivery were going to make a big killin' together, make a muckin' fortune they were! Till Kontannis killed Ivery.'

'Did he? Why?'

'Ah, come on now. Greed. What's better'n fifty per cent?' He laughed. 'I'll tell you: a hundred per cent.'

'Clapp,' I said.

'What?'

'Clapp. He talked, up in Kendal. To MacDown. He talked about Ivery. Why? I mean, if he *knew* who had the negatives all along, why didn't you all go straight for Ivery?'

'Because,' Lemmon said, 'what Clapp knew, we, the rest of us, didn't. All right? Clapp was goin' to play it on his own. He was all set to head south from Kendal, when the cops turned up. His mouthpiece told us—his solicitor. Clapp's bad luck, not ours. He's the one that got nicked, and that bein' so, he talked to save his own skin.' Lemmon spat. 'It won't get him any place at all, it won't. Grassin' never does, no matter what the cops promise. One day, we're goin' to get Mister Clapp, see if we don't!'

'You can have him,' I said, 'but I've a feeling you're going to be inside a lot longer than Clapp, once MacDown gets his hands on you.'

Lemmon laughed. 'That'll be the day.'

A thought struck me. I asked, 'Where did you find the body?'

'Ivery's? Under the cellar bricks in Kontannis's lousy shop. It wasn't difficult. Kontannis hadn't done a very good job. Any jack'd have found the stiff, if one had gone along to look.

'Where's Kontannis now?'

Lemmon jerked a hand backwards. I couldn't see what he was pointing at, that part of the van was too dark, but he helped me out with his torch. 'Dead, like Ivery,' he said. 'Remember what I said about a hundred per cent?' He laughed. I wondered how much further the field was due to be narrowed. There were still Peacock and Phillips left. Or I supposed they were still around. At any rate, somebody was driving the van.

I asked, 'Where are we going now, Lemmon?'

'Well,' he said, 'you could call it a disposal run. We've got two bodies to be got rid of. Plus.'

'Plus what?'

I wasn't being very bright. Lemmon sounded thoroughly impatient when he said, 'Soon there'll be three—won't there?'

I said, feeling sick as the van swayed, but sick with more than just that swaying motion and the blow on my head, 'I take your point, but if I were you I wouldn't be too sure. You haven't answered my question, anyway. *Where* are we going?'

'You'll see. Curiosity killed the cat, dinnit?'

Lemmon guffawed. He fancied himself as a wit, today. He seemed very happy. I took this, unhappy myself, as a sign of confidence. I tried to remind myself that confidence was sometimes qualified by the adjective over-weening. Not very successfully, however. There was something basically genuine about Lemmon's optimism. He had never exactly said he had the negatives in the van, but that was the feeling I had. So near, and yet so far! I wondered if specimens had already gone off to Downing Street, as a reminder. Lemmon didn't say anything more after that; he flicked off his torch and started humming to himself, some pop tune it was. Ivery's body kept on lurching into me, flaccidly. Gradually the angle shifted to the sway of the van, and once when the torch came back on briefly I saw the lolling head. Ivery had been a good deal younger than Phyllis Marton—early twenties, that dead face looked like. So probably her cousin was younger too, if this dead man had been that cousin's husband.

I wondered what Lemmon and his friends had lined up for me. I began to feel the terrible pressure of time, like a physical force on its own. There wasn't long to go for the blackmailers; there must be less long to go for me.

Nevertheless, we drove a long way. Of course, I didn't know the direction; but quite soon it had become obvious enough that we were clear of London's traffic. Now we were going along really fast; but it wasn't a motorway, because we slowed at times, and at other times stopped, as if waiting at lights or giving way at a roundabout. I thought, if only somebody would smash into us! Not too hard, of course. But hard enough. Two ready-made corpses and a bound man would look a little odd to the rubberneckers. But that sort of luck never does happen.

It seemed to me a long, long time later when the van slowed again and then made a very sharp left turn. Going dead slow now, we lurched and bumped for a while and then came to what turned out to be final rest. Lemmon moved to the doors at the back and swung them open, and jumped down. It was the very dead of night—very dark, no moon at all. No light anywhere. There was a smell of fields, and of damp rising from earth, and somewhere a night bird called, eerie and remote. Lemmon went round to the front, and evidently climbed into the van with the driver, for there was a small lurch and a door clicked shut, and then I heard low voices, though I couldn't catch what they were saying. About ten minutes later, I think, Lemmon came back. He said, 'You're goin' to get down. I'm goin' to untie your ankles, but don't start nothin', all right? I got a gun.'

A gun would be better by far than another well and I said so.

'There's no well,' Lemmon said.

'What then?'

'For now anyway—nothin'.'

I said, 'You've already told me, I'm going to be the third body.'

'Maybe you can avoid it, Mister Cane.'

'How?'

'By doin' what we tell you.'

I jeered. 'You expect me to belive anything *you* say, Lemmon? I co-operate, and I get my reward? Like hell I do!'

He said with full seriousness, 'It's your only chance, innit? I mean, either you do as I say and hope we'll keep our promise, or you don't do as I say and you *definitely* end up dead. Get my meaning?'

'Yes, I get it,' I said bitterly. I looked at Ivery's body, visible in the small beam of a pencil flash that Lemmon was using to keep me in view. As the beam flickered aside I saw Kontannis as well. He was not a pleasant sight; he had been done over very, very thoroughly before he died. I suppose Lemmon had given me that sight of Kontannis deliberately. If so, he achieved his objective. Any chance was better than none. I said, 'All right. What do you want me to do?'

'You'll see,' Lemmon answered briefly. 'First, you get down. Then we go for a

walk. You'll get your detailed orders then.'
He leaned forward towards my feet with a
knife in his left hand. He used the blade
on the ropes by touch, keeping his gaze
and his torch beam on my face and his
gun steady in his right hand. I saw that
it was a revolver, not an automatic, and
it carried a silencer. When my feet were
free, but not my hands, I was told to
get out. I slid towards the tail end of
the van, and sat for a moment with
my legs dangling. Lemmon put his foot
against my backside, and shoved, and out
I went, landing in a heap on dampish earth
covered with twigs and small broken pieces
of wood.

Lemmon laughed coarsely and said, 'Get
up.' I did so, feeling sour to the stomach
with anger and fatigue and the recent
close proximity of the dead. Lemmon
was using his torch, so I assumed with
a fair degree of certainty that we were
a good distance from any habitation. In
that tiny beam of light I saw trees. Plenty
of them. The van had been pulled into
a clearing, not far in from the road—a
country road it must be, I thought, and
little used. Certainly there were no traffic
sounds, no lights. But we turned past the

van, in which I could just make out the hunched figure of the driver behind the wheel, and headed away from the road, going deeper into the woods. There was a track running through, but it had a disused feel, and after only a dozen or so yards I found I was keeping my head down to avoid the sting and lash of twigs and branches, and I felt the occasional rip of brambles across my flesh and clothing. Lemmon clumped along close behind me; I heard his heavy breathing, and now and again he gave me a sharp prod with his revolver, just to make sure I knew it was still there.

Once, he asked, 'Know where you are, do you?'

'No,' I said. I thought he was going to tell me at last, but I was wrong. He said it wouldn't be long now before I found out; and I had to leave it at that. To my mind, it was all very like a couple of nights earlier, up north on the Ottershaw property, only this time I was in a much worse position and with no apparent hope of ever getting out of it again.

After, I think, about another fifteen minutes' walking and shoving through the overgrown wood Lemmon's torch, probing a little ahead, showed the end of the trees. At once Lemmon flicked the beam off, and at the same time told me to stop. He said, 'We go across a field now. Two fields. Then we come to a road. Along it, there'll be a phone box. You'll be goin' into it, and you'll make a call. I'll be with you, nice and close. You'll say what you're told, and no more. If you try any tricks, I cut the call at once and we leave the box—we'll have plenty of time to get away. After that, Mister Cane, you'll be considered to have stopped co-operatin' and death won't come easy. See?'

'Too much melodrama,' I said. 'Lemmon, you're corny.'

'It doesn't worry me, doesn't that,' he said smugly. 'I've got you right where I want you, and don't you be daft enough to forget it.' He added, 'If you're thinkin' I'm goin' to untie your hands to make the call, you can think again, because I'm not. I'll dial, and I'll hold the receiver for you.'

'Who am I going to call?' I asked.

But for some reason he still wouldn't tell me that. Retrospectively, I think

229

perhaps he didn't want to provoke a stiffer resistance, or perhaps he saw a psychological advantage in holding it until I was actually presented with the ringing tone at the other end—but at the time I just didn't know. He told me to get moving again then, and I did, and we came out from the trees, and I still had no idea in the world where we were. All along, I'd been trying to figure it. I only had a time-estimation to go on, and that told me we had to be a long way out of London. It was no help, because we could be in any geographical direction—and really I couldn't even be sure of any true estimate of net distance from London, since a night arrival could have been necessary to Lemmon and we could simply have been detouring so as to fill in time.

Leaving the trees, we started across the first of the two fields. It was much easier going now, though the field was rough and pitted with rabbit burrows, and it was still very dark, with no light anywhere to break that pitch darkness, not even Lemmon's torch. I wondered how Lemmon could be sure of his direction, and soon I found he wasn't so sure, because he directed me left and we came to a hedge. 'We'll follow this round,' he said. 'We should come to a gate.'

'We'll go through the gate?'

'I'll tell you when we get there.'

God, but he was a suspicious-minded bastard. He couldn't even give that much away in advance. I was astonished he'd even mentioned the gate at all! Maybe it just slipped out.

Something clicked in my head: it was like a revelation. I thought: *just slipped out!*

Something, or somebody, else could slip, too: me.

My heart pounded. I walked on, maybe another twenty or thirty yards. Lemmon was still nice and close behind me.

I shoved my foot into the first rabbit hole it contacted after that, and I stopped, very suddenly. Lemmon lurched up closer, but stopped himself just in time. I cursed under my breath; I wouldn't get a second chance at this. I slid to the ground, to try it another way, and probably, in fact, a better way.

I gave a yelp as of intense pain.

Lemmon said, 'Get up.'

I said, 'I can't. I've twisted my ankle. In fact I think it's broken. It's your fault, you bloody fool. If you'd untied my hands I could have saved myself.'

'Never mind the muckin' excuses,' he snarled. He was starting to panic already, I felt—I must be pretty vital to the plans. 'Get up and walk!'

I made more sad noises of agony. 'It's no good,' I said. 'I can't, I just can't.' I rolled over on to my back, and brought a foot up and waggled it towards Lemmon. 'Take a look,' I said. 'See for yourself, if you don't believe me.'

Swearing viciously, Lemmon flicked on his torch. That was helpful of him—very. I could line myself up on him beautifully, and I did. As he bent to take a look I pulled the other foot back like lightning and then slammed them both straight into his jaw. There was a lovely crump of breaking bone and loosening teeth and Lemmon vanished from sight as the torch zipped off into space and lay with its light shining at the hedge. I was on my feet by this time, searching for Lemmon. I soon found him, although he was out cold, because I almost fell over again when I walked on his unresistant body. I could only see him as a blur in the darkness, but I could make out his face more easily as a whitish splodge.

I stood near the face and lifted my foot, and I brought it down time and time again on his head. I kicked hard behind the ear with the point of my shoe. It was vicious, but Lemmon, child rapist, child murderer, was a vicious beast, and the only way to deal with a vicious beast was viciously. And he had to stay unconscious until I found help, and came back, and had him brought in. To me then, as I think to MacDown secretly all along, the arrest of Lemmon was a damn sight more important than the peace of mind of the Prime Minister.

When Lemmon must have been all but dead, I left him and continued fast along the hedge until I found the gate. It was shut, and, with my hands still securely tied, I had the devil's own job climbing over it, but I managed. I managed by getting to the top and then throwing myself down the other side. I landed heavily, but not disastrously, picked myself up and hurried on, feeling against all reason that Lemmon might be behind me, rampaging on for the kill. In fact, of course, there was no pursuit. Still keeping against the hedge, I went on, and in due course I found another gate, and beyond it I could make out the whiteness of a dusty country road. Again the gate was shut, and again I went into my throwing-over act, landing much more painfully this time, on the hard road.

I looked around. It was still as dark as ever and I still had no idea where I was. I didn't even know which way along that road to go, and it was just luck that sent me in the right direction. I walked for quite a long way, I don't know how far it was, before I saw the loom of cottages ahead. Even then I didn't recognize the place.

Then I saw the telephone box that Lemmon had said I would find. I made for it, and went in. There was no light, or anyway it wasn't working, but I peered closely at the number written up on the dialling instruction board. Public call boxes could give a lost man a direction, couldn't they? They could; and this one did. After a lot of close eye work I just made out the exchange name: Staveley. That rang a pretty clanging bell and I didn't like the sound of it, taken in conjunction with the fact I was supposed to have made a call from here. Bill Crimond's number was a Staveley one. So, if I wasn't actually in Drayling, I was undoubtedly in the close vicinity.

Why? What went on now?

I leaned back against the glass, trying to think this thing out sensibly. I was to have made a phone call, with Lemmon breathing down my neck. Whoever I was to ring had to hear my voice, not Lemmon's, so they had to be someone who would know me. Phyllis Marton—had she come back here to Drayling Hall, and did Lemmon know this?

I just didn't know, but then it came to me that possibly whoever I was to call would have *trusted* me, and that I was to lead them into danger of some sort...because of that implicit trust.

And the only ones who would really fill that bill around here would be Bill and Eve—and I couldn't see how it could be them. Maybe I should ring them and try to sound something out, only I couldn't, not with my hands tied. I pushed my way out of the call box. Now that I was mentally orientated towards some idea of my whereabouts, I was soon able to tick over and establish a landmark or two; and I realized I was in fact right there—in Drayling. I made for the village bobby's house, fast.

CHAPTER TEN

'Sounded like you was *kicking* the door,' the constable said in an aggrieved voice. He was bleary-eyed and stubbly and showing a lot of chest hair through the open neck of his pyjamas.

I said, I was, as a matter of fact—'

'No manners,' the constable broke in. 'Good mind to book you for damage to property—'

'I couldn't help it,' I said loudly. 'Look—no hands!' I turned round, then I swivelled back to face him. He looked a real picture; this sort of thing didn't happen often in villages, I'll bet. 'How about untying me?'

'Who tied you up?' he asked dazedly.

'Not the arm of the law,' I said, 'and not a law-abiding citizen either. May I come in?'

236

'All right,' he said, and opened the door wider. 'Now, who are you, and what are you doing like this at this time of the night, may I ask?' He banged the door behind me, and closed the neck of his pyjamas. A more official look came into his eye.

I said, 'The name's Cane, Captain Cane, and I can give you a number in London to ring so you can confirm to your entire satisfaction that I'm acting for a certain department of the law. But you'll have to hurry.' I put quite a lot of regimental bull into my voice and I saw the result germinating in the constable's manner.

He said, 'I'll do whatever's necessary sir, but I'll have to ask for some explanation to go on first.'

'Sorry,' I said. 'It'll take far too long. Please get on the line to London.' I gave him Limbrick's number. 'There's a man lying outside the village, in a field. I can guide you to him and we may reach him before he either dies or is picked up by a bunch of armed men who're causing rather a lot of worry to Downing Street. I repeat, there's a need for speed.' I paused, feeling desperate in the face of thick-headedness. 'I dare say

237

you like your nice, quiet little job in Drayling?'

'Exactly what do you mean by that, sir?' he asked, his face hardening.

With deliberation I said, 'I mean I'm bloody well threatening you with being bloody well disciplined unless you pull your finger out and bloody well get cracking!'

After Limbrick had okayed me—I had spoken personally to Limbrick and told him the score so far as I knew it—that bobby couldn't do enough. He virtually girded himself for battle; he was no youngster, and it turned out he'd done three years in an infantry regiment before joining the Force, and he started to feel all soldierly again, as though he was going out on a mission with his company commander. My idea was to lose no time in bringing Lemmon in, but first of all I used the bobby's phone to call the Crimond's number and I got Eve. I got her much sooner than I'd expected, almost as though she had been sitting by the phone, and that worried me for a start.

She sounded desperately frightened. At first she didn't even take in who I was. I said, 'Eve, listen. It's me—John Cane.

238

What on earth's up?'

'Oh, *John!*' The relief, the sheer gladness, was overwhelming; I felt even more worried and alarmed. 'John, where are you?'

'In Drayling,' I said. 'In the police station.'

'Oh!' she said. 'I was just this minute going to ring Mr Appleby. Just this very minute, isn't that funny—'

She seemed to me to be babbling, so I cut in sharply. 'Now listen, Eve. Calm down, dear, and tell me what the trouble is. Why were you going to ring the police, at this time of the night? And where's Bill?'

She said, 'That's one of the awful things, John. Bill's not here—'

'Where is he?'

'I—I don't know. He went out earlier, much earlier. He wouldn't say where he was going...he was in rather a temper, actually. We hadn't had a row, but he'd, well, sort of worked himself up...'

'What about?'

'I don't *know*, John! He just seemed to *want* to quarrel. And he hasn't come back. I never thought he'd be out for long, just a drink at the Rose and Crown perhaps, but—'

'Has he been there?'

'No. I rang to ask. But John–'

'What time did he go out?'

'Just after eight. John, listen, please.' There was a dreadful urgency in her voice, and it suddenly lowered, as though what she was about to say mustn't be overheard. 'John, I'm almost certain there's someone lurking about outside—'

'*What!*' I almost shouted down the line. 'No, don't repeat it, Eve, I did hear. Can you add anything? Who you think it is, what they're doing, how long they've been there?'

She said, 'I've no idea who it could be or why, nor how long it's been going on. I heard a sound downstairs about a quarter of an hour ago...I was lying awake worrying about Bill.'

'Anyone entering?'

'No. Not that sort of sound. I should have said *outside* rather than downstairs. Like someone knocking over a flower pot, that sort of thing.'

'You didn't go down?'

'No—'

'Nor put on any lights?'

'Not then. I have, now. When the phone went. I thought it might be Bill.'

'All right,' I said. 'If there's anyone there, they may have heard the phone ringing in any case, so don't worry about it now. Put the light out when you ring off, and get dressed—in the dark. Don't do anything else. How are the children?'

'Asleep,' she said. 'Thank God.'

'Right,' I told her, 'I'm on my way. Just go on keeping your head, Eve. You've done fine so far.'

I rang off. I gave the constable, Appleby, the facts. I said, 'We'll have to leave the man in the field for now. What transport have you?'

'I've a Panda car, sir. Morris 1000.'

'Better get it on the road,' I said.

'It'd be less obvious to walk, sir. It's no real distance.'

'I intend to walk, myself. I'd like you to follow in the Panda, after say fifteen minutes. We may need it for a chase.'

'You mean to go in on your own?' he asked.

'As a start, yes. I'd like more men around soonest possible. Can you fix that?'

The policeman nodded. 'I'll ring through to Huntingdon at once,' he said.

'Thanks a lot. You might mention that these men are armed and will be fairly

241

desperate when cornered. I can assure you, they'll shoot their way through if they can. My advice would be, all police should carry revolvers.'

'They don't like that, at County,' Appleby said as he picked up his telephone. I left him to sort it out. I'd always heard the police didn't like being armed, but I wondered how accurate that really was, if the real truth might be that the brass didn't like the responsibility of giving the order. I'd have bet any money the ordinary copper felt a damn sight safer when he was on a level with the villains, defence-wise. As for me that night, I had no option but to go in without a gun, and I didn't like it at all. I wished I'd had my hands free so I could have picked up Lemmon's gun back in that field, but that was water under the bridge by now.

Dove Cottage wasn't more than a quarter of a mile at the most from the bobby's house and by now my geography, aided by an ordnance survey map I had discovered in Appleby's hall, had come back to me. There was no sign of the dawn yet and I doubted if I would be spotted as I ran silently past the Rose and Crown, all shut up for the night and sleeping. The

Crimonds' little place was up a narrow lane leading off the main street of the village. It wasn't the only cottage in that lane, but it was rather out on a limb as it were, isolated at the far end. There was some building work in progress between it and the nearest neighbours lower down, I remembered. Bungalows, at least one of them with four walls already up. That could make a reasonable place to hide in, and watch, or reasonable cover to do a bunk to when the shooting started. On the other hand, somebody else could have had that idea as well.

Suddenly I wondered what the hell I was going to do. I had no plan, just a determination to go to Eve's help. It wasn't really enough, on its own. I might even make things worse; I might precipitate something.

I stopped, just past the Rose and Crown, full of indecision. It came to me that it wouldn't be any use going up the lane; whoever was hanging around the house would be bound to hear me coming. True, there was a grass verge, in places, but when I hit the hard surface that would be it.

A frontal assault, I fancied, was out.

I visualized that copper's map. A little

243

way ahead of me there was another lane...running more or less parallel with the Crimonds', I remembered. I hadn't been up that way during my brief visit earlier, but I felt there was sure to be a way through. I would probably have to cross someone else's garden but I wasn't terribly worried about trespass. I should have a better chance that way.

I went on, and turned up the first lane. I couldn't wait to jump the bastard that was scaring the life out of Eve. As I went along I tried to reason things out, to get some idea of what the set-up was. It seemed more and more likely that it was the Crimonds I had been supposed to ring under instructions from Lemmon. This, I began to accept as a fact; but I couldn't fit it in, I couldn't see the connexion. Unless it was just Peacock's way of ensuring my help. Say I was to have spoken to Eve and given her some yarn that would have brought her out of the cottage, because she trusted me, and then Lemmon would have got his dirty clutches on her and she would have been hustled back through the woods to the van? But what would the purpose have been? To use her as a hostage, presumably. To use her against me? But I didn't see what help I could have been to Peacock at this stage. He had the negatives, hadn't he, or rather Lemmon had?

But then *had* he? That had never been said, in so many words. I had just assumed it. Surely Peacock didn't *still* believe I had them cached away somewhere?

And anyway—if the idea had been to draw Eve out into the open to be set up for capture—what was Bill supposed to be doing in the meantime? Letting her go out, alone, into the night, on my say-so? Of course, he trusted me too, I knew that—but still! He'd see it as a trifle dicey, I'd have thought.

Or did Lemmon know that Bill wasn't at home?

No, that would be impossible. He'd only gone out at eight o'clock, according to Eve. At that time, we must have been on the road.

I gave it up. I had a strong feeling it was all going to be sorted out quite soon now anyway. I was well up the lane by this time and looking out for a way through that would bring me out as close as possible to the Crimonds' cottage. I decided I had found it when I came to a small belt of trees between two cottages, running clear in the direction I wanted. I seemed fated, I thought, to operate in trees. I didn't like the past associations all that much, but it couldn't be helped. I had just entered the belt, which couldn't be all that long, when I heard a car's engine. It was coming from the direction of the bobby's house, and I judged from the sound that it had now turned up the Crimonds' lane.

I put on speed. My intention had been to be *in situ* and in action long before Appleby made it. But as I neared the lane I saw I'd been mistaken and it wasn't PC Appleby. The car was no Panda. I was sure of that, even though it had its lights switched off. It was long and sleek and I was pretty sure it was a Daimler Jag. If so, it could be Peacock, but if it was, I still couldn't for the very life of me see why, unless they expected to pick me up there.

I watched.

A shadow came away from the side of Dove Cottage, approaching the car. I heard a voice. It sounded, and this could have been imagination just then, like Phillips, Clapp's twin skinhead. He was reporting all quiet, so far as I could hear, and the bird intact. That would be Eve. I couldn't catch the reply from inside the Jag, but I lost all interest in replies just then, because I had heard another car in the distance and knew that this time it had to be Appleby, driving, very likely, to his death.

It was Appleby, all right. The little Panda was coming up the lane, with its POLICE sign all lit up. I didn't think that was very clever of Appleby, really. I'd have come up like the Jag, all lights doused. I hadn't even time to come out and yell a warning. The Panda's headlamps beamed straight on to the Jag and I saw three men inside. One of them fired immediately, straight through the rear window. I saw the Panda swerve on to the grass verge and stop, with its lights still full on. I heard one of its doors come open.

Then I heard a shout from the Jag: 'Inside, Phillips. You know where to go, after.' Then the Jag moved a little ahead, swung towards the Crimonds' drive-in, turned, backed, presumably to give itself room to increase speed fast, then went forward. It went ahead like a bullet, no lights, heading to zoom past the beached Panda, and all I heard was one terrible scream and then it was gone.

When I reached him, poor Appleby was stone dead in the road and was barely recognizable. I was tremendously and uselessly sorry I'd been rude to him. There was absolutely nothing I could do there, so I ran back for Dove Cottage. As I went I heard the shatter of glass. A window, no doubt, providing ingress for Mr Phillips. I could imagine Eve's fear now; I could imagine far too much.

I belted into the little garden and ran round the cottage. I found the broken window and I went in fast. I heard crying from upstairs. The children, not Eve. Then I heard Eve's voice, high, piercing, hysterical.

'Leave me alone! Leave me alone!' After that, as I padded up the stairs, silence; silence followed by a low moaning sound, and again Eve's voice pleading with Phillips. 'No, no, please, don't do it, please,' and then dreadful sobbing.

I reached the open doorway of Eve's bedroom. There was a light on now, and I saw Phillips holding Eve, standing with his hand moving over her body. His back was towards me—and his head. He never heard a thing, and I fixed my attention on his head, and outside the room still, I picked up something I remembered Bill bringing back from Aden. A carved wooden figure, an Indian holy man, thick and strong and heavy. I went in with this in my hand, looking intently at that cropped skinhead, and what Phillips was doing to Eve. I thought of Appleby, lying out there in the road. Phillips was far too busy, far too engrossed in his desires, to hear anything and in fact I dare say he died happy. He certainly died messily, and without so much as a murmur. He dropped like a log and I caught Eve as she fell into my arms. She had fainted, and I carried her to the bed, and laid her down gently. I smoothed her hair from her face, went to the basin and soaked my handkerchief in cold water and laid it on her forehead. The children were crying, worse than ever. I left Eve and went to their bedroom They hadn't come out; Eve had probably told them not to, whatever happened, and I expect they had been too frightened anyway after Phillips broke in.

I told them everything was going to be all right.

'Mummy's fine,' I said. 'Tired, but fine. You must let her sleep. I'll look after her. You know me, don't you?'

'Yes.' This was the boy, David. 'You're a friend of daddy's.'

'That's right,' I said. 'A soldier. You've got to be a soldier, too, haven't you, David, till daddy gets back to take over.'

He nodded stoutly, though puffy-eyed from crying. 'Yes,' he said. Then, 'Where is daddy?'

I couldn't answer that. I said, 'Oh, he'll be back soon, David. Now I must go and look after mummy. You'll be all right, won't you, and look after your sister?'

'Yes,' he said again. I went back across the small landing, opening a cupboard on the way and finding a sheet. I draped it over Phillips. I was desperately worried. Suddenly, I didn't like the implications for Bill. God alone knew where Bill had gone, why he had run out, in a sense, on his wife, gone off with no explanation. I had to talk to Eve before I did anything else—or almost. There was just one thing, in fact: I had to report to the police, so they could get after the Jag. I went to the phone. It was dead. Phillips had probably cut the wires on entry. The police would have to wait. I couldn't leave Dove Cottage just now, to go down to the little village station—and Appleby's wife.

After a few minutes Eve came round, caught her breath, and looked at me with wide, terrified eyes.

'It's all right, I said. 'It's me—John. No more worries now, Eve dear.'

'That man—'

'Gone,' I said quickly. I would need to keep her away from the sheeted bundle on the floor till Phillips had been scraped up. 'Forget about him—it's over, all over. And the children are okay. David's in charge—the soldier, in daddy's absence. I'll bet he's feeling really important.' I paused. 'Eve, what about Bill? Can you add anything to what you told me on the phone? It's important.'

She said, 'I can't, John. It's all I know.'

'You're worried about him, aren't you?'

'Of course I am. How can I not be?'

'I know,' I said. I bent and took her face in my hands; her long fair hair streamed down over my wrists. 'I didn't mean quite that. I meant...well, you've been worried before, haven't you? Or haven't you?'

'No,' she said, looking at me blankly. 'Never. Oh, of course I have been when he's been overseas, but that's different, isn't it?'

I said, 'Yes, it is, and it's not what I meant.'

'Well, what *do* you mean?'

'Never mind,' I said, and I grinned down at her. 'I don't know what I mean, and that's honest. Only I wish Bill would come back before the police get here.'

'Do we need the police?' It sounded crazy, but she didn't know Phillips and Appleby were dead and I knew what she meant; the scandal, in a village, could be a kind of death in itself. A woman with a man in her bedroom, an alleged assault, no smoke without fire, that sort of thing, the stupid, idle, malicious tongues that would wag in and around the Rose and Crown. A woman whose husband was away a lot and who could have had an army quarter if she'd really wanted to be with him—oh yes, I could hear all that ringing in my ears! But I had to tell her the truth, even while she was still upset, because the men from County headquarters would be coming in at any moment. I said, 'Eve dear, the police are already in on this. From London to the Yorkshire Dales and back again. It's not just a case of a man hanging round your house at night. I can't tell you the whole thing—not yet. But it's really big, Eve.'

'But why me? Why do I get involved? Through you, John?'

I said, 'Yes. I'm sorry.'

She put her hands up to her head. She was very white and drawn, and her face was all puffy from crying, just like her children, but there was a curious intensity in her expression, as though she was puzzling something out. I knew what she was going to say next, and she did. She said, 'And Bill.'

'How d'you mean?'

'Through Bill too. Isn't that right, John? That's why there's been—all this, tonight, and what you said about the police, and it being big? Bill's involved too, in some way?'

I said, 'I don't know, Eve, I really don't.'

'No,' she said, and her eyes were haggard now, 'but you're thinking it, aren't you?'

'I don't know what to think.'

She closed her eyes and gave a deep shuddering sigh. 'Well, what's next?' she asked after a moment.

I was about to answer when, for the third time that night, I heard a car coming. I heard the scream of tyres as it braked on its driver sighting PC Appleby. I went to the window and looked out. I saw the blue light flashing. 'It's the police,' I said. 'The police from Huntingdon. I'm sorry, Eve. You'll have to answer some questions now.'

'All right,' she said. 'do you want to go down and meet them? I'll be all right now.'

So I went down and opened up the front door. The car had pulled on past Appleby, and another was coming in behind it. A uniformed inspector, long and lean like a rasher of bacon, came towards me. 'Captain Cane?' he asked.

'Right. How did you know?'

'Does it matter?' he said irritably. I dare say he'd been shaken by seeing Appleby. 'What's going on here, Captain Cane?'

I told him. 'Mrs Crimond's all right, more or less. You'll find a dead man up in her bedroom, name of Phillips. One of Peacock's mob—you'll have heard?'

'Yes. Who killed this man?'

'I did.'

He pushed past me, into the hall. 'I'd better take a look,' he said. He darted up the stairs. Behind him a sergeant and three constables, and two plain-clothes men, entered the hall. One of the plain-clothes men asked if I wished to make a statement, and I said, no, I didn't, not yet, since I preferred to report to my own superior officer first. He didn't seem to mind. I asked him if anybody had happened to pick up a Daimler Jag; and very much to my surprise he said they had.

'Just beyond Eaton Socon on the A1,' he said. 'Heading south, very fast. There was a running battle.'

'Guns?'

'Guns,' he said.

'How did you know?'

'About the Jag? PC Appleby used his pocket radio. He passed the registration number, then went off the air. We guessed why.' He shrugged, but his face looked immensely sad. 'So we had to get the Jag, didn't we, Captain Cane?'

I said, 'Sure. And thank God you did! Who did you bring in?'

'Peacock and Clapp were two of the names. I don't know the other. He was dead, anyway.'

'I suppose,' I asked, not taking in the odd fact of Clapp being out of the Kendal nick, 'you don't happen to know the whereabouts of Major Crimond?'

'I was going to ask you that,' the man said. 'You've had your crack of the whip. It's me who's supposed to be the detective around here.'

'My apologies,' I said, and at that moment the uniformed officer called down the stairs for me. I went up. Nodding through the bedroom door towards Phillips he said, 'I'll have to know the circumstances from you. I realize your standing in this matter, of course, but you'll see my point.'

'Of course,' I said. I gave him all the facts. 'Mrs Crimond will corroborate all that.'

'She has, in advance. I've already taken her statement.' He waved a notebook at me. 'I don't think we'll need you any more tonight, Captain Cane. I'd be obliged if you'd report to County headquarters at 1000 hours precisely.'

I stared at him. 'Just a minute,' I said angrily. 'I'm a friend of the family, you know. Besides, I have a job to do. I intend staying right here—if you don't mind!'

He seemed about to argue, but stopped before he was fully launched and, looking impatient, went to the banisters and stared down, because some sort of dispute seemed to be going on in the hall. A small dishevelled figure was pushing its way through the crowd of policemen. I was extremely surprised to see him, but also much relieved. The inspector asked in a hectoring tone, 'Who are you, may I ask?'

'Chief Superintendent MacDown of the Special Branch. I may come up, I take it, and consult my colleague?'

'Of course, sir,' The inspector was deflated. Smiling, MacDown climbed the stairs. He reached the landing, and laid a hand on my arm. 'I thought I'd find you here, laddie,' he said. 'You've done well. I'm proud of you. I shall say the same thing to Mr Limbrick.'

I said, 'You sound as if it's all over, Mr MacDown.'

'Oh, it is, laddie, it is. Here.' He fished in his pocket and brought out a brown manilla envelope. 'Take a look at that.'

I did so. It was the negatives. Looking pleased with himself MacDown said, 'Aye, it's all over. The Prime Minister is sleeping easy now. I've already telephoned direct to Downing Street.'

I said, 'Well, I suppose you're going to explain?'

'Of course.' He took my arm again. 'Where's the lady?'

'Mrs Crimond?' I gestured towards Eve's room. 'In there.'

'Then we'll go downstairs again,' Mac-Down said. He turned away and I followed. So did the inspector. We went into the sitting-room. MacDown sat himself in an easy chair and rubbed at his eyes. He looked immensely old and tired. He said, 'I had a little luck. Clapp said rather more than he thought.'

'Clapp!' I said, suddenly remembering what the plain-clothes man had told me. 'He was in the Jag when they intercepted it!'

MacDown nodded. 'That's correct, I understand. I let him go, you see. It's an old trick, but it seldom fails. The criminal mind, the *lower* criminal mind, is really extremely unoriginal, Mr Cane. He rejoined his associates, it seems, and—'

'Or the other way round, could be. I rather gathered Clapp's associates had plans for him. They just hadn't got around to putting them into effect.'

MacDown nodded. 'Aye, maybe. Anyhow,

I was elsewhere at the time of the interception. *I* found a van drawn into a small wood—'

'I don't know about small,' I said. 'I walked right through it. But do go on! Are you telling me you were behind us?'

'Quite correct,' MacDown said. 'It is easy to maintain a tail in the dark if you keep a decent distance and don't use lights. I wished to let things take their expected course, up to a certain point. They failed to do so in *every* particular, but I did stumble across a gentleman named Lemmon, whom I have wanted, as you know, for some time—'

'Stumbled across him, did you?' I interrupted. 'That was a dead lucky break, in that damn great field in the dark—'

'No, no, no, merely observation. You see, the man had dropped a torch, which was still shining its light to heaven—and to inquisitive police officers.' MacDown placed the tips of his fingers together parsonically and stared over them at me. 'Lemmon was in poor shape, but perhaps you know that, Mr Cane?'

'Yes,' I said, 'I did know that. Will he live?'

'Frankly, I have my doubts, but if he does he will duly go down for a very long time. It's most satisfactory.'

'And the negatives? Where did they turn up? I was assuming Lemmon had them—was that the case?'

'Aye, it was. They were in the van.'

'Then why was he coming here, why all tonight's business?'

MacDown said, 'I haven't Lemmon's own story. So far, he has not been fit to talk—but he will, he will, if he lives. Not that it matters now. I have the whole story pieced together already.' He looked up at the ceiling for a moment, and there was real sorrow and concern in his face, so that I knew, with a strange certainty now, what was coming. Bill. 'Poor, poor lady. Its always the innocents who suffer, Mr Cane. I am always depressed by that, it takes the pleasure out of a job otherwise well done.'

I felt jagged and on edge. 'What did he do?' I asked.

MacDown said, 'I'm sorry to say that he as well as Harold Marton was having an affair with Robert Marton's wife. A very advanced and permissive one—photography came into it. A three-some—if you follow. Though this, Harold

Marton did not know.'

'You mean—'

'I mean your friend was the photographer.'

'Good God!' I said. 'Why?'

MacDown shrugged. 'Because it gave him a thrill, and because he saw a chance of making a good deal of money. Mrs Marton made the suggestion of blackmail, you see, and promised him a generous financial reward. Then, you see, he saw an opportunity of even more money, and he made a mistake. He put the squeeze on Peacock—just within the last twenty-four hours, this was. A very foolish man. He tried to play off Ottershaw against Peacock as well, which was even more foolish. However, Peacock humoured him—promised agreement to his terms. We, who know better, would not have taken that promise at its face value—would we?'

I said, 'No—I suppose not.' I was recalling how Phyllis Marton had refused to give me the name of the man who had actually taken the photographs. She had obviously been shielding him. I wondered if she had genuinely loved him in her own way; after all, she was a woman as Limbrick had said and she could have done so, whatever her other motives and involvements. I remembered that night in the Rose and Crown, remembered the looks that had been exchanged. I suppose I should have had an inkling before now...I came back to the present and said, 'But the—photographer did believe Peacock?' I don't know why we were keeping off naming names, but it was mutual, and it may have been because we both felt a sense of poignancy in sitting there in that room, with Eve upstairs, and the children waiting, and we were inhibited by a common sense of decency and the fitness of things. 'He took Peacock's word?'

'Yes, and went to meet him tonight. Your part was—this is mere supposition, based upon circumstantial evidence—your part was to extract the lady from the cottage. You see?'

'To be a hostage and a guarantee,' I said in a low voice. 'I worked that out for myself, afterwards, though I didn't know the actual reason.' I paused. 'How did you find out the rest, Mr MacDown?'

He said, 'Because I found our friend, Mr Cane. I went back to the van after finding Lemmon, you see, and I watched what happened, and I interfered. But too late.'

'He was dead?'

'No. Not then. He talked, Mr Cane. He told me the lot, and then he died. You'll be glad to know I have arrested the man who killed him. The murderer went some while since to a cell in Peterborough.' He glanced apologetically at the Huntingdon inspector. 'I have friends in that force,' he said. 'I'll need special facilities for speaking to the man in the morning. You'll not mind, I'm sure.' He turned to me again then. 'Go upstairs and talk to the lady,' he said quietly. 'Mind what you say, Mr Cane. The Official Secrets Act applies still. There's virtue in that. There are certain things that I both can and will see to. The proceedings will in any event be held *in camera*. You will say nothing to the lady about any photography.'

I got there. 'You mean—?'

'Yes,' MacDown said quickly. 'That is exactly what I do mean. I'm willing to strike a bargain, to talk terms with villains—when I am utterly convinced that justice would be better served thereby. Even though certain guilty persons will get away with it.' I took that as an oblique reference to Phyllis Marton, and probably Ottershaw. 'And I have more than enough authority to bring it off,' MacDown went on, 'and I trust the inspector will also bear in mind the Official Secrets Act.'

The inspector coughed and turned his lips down. He didn't approve, but he would value his career. I said, 'Thank you, Mr MacDown. I really mean that with all my heart.' I added, 'It's been a pleasure, in many ways, to work with you, Chief Superintendent.'

He raised an eyebrow. 'I hope the use of the past tense is not intentional, Mr Cane?'

I took a deep, deep breath and blew it out again. 'Oh yes it is,' I said, and I got to my feet and went upstairs, past the weary policemen waiting in the hall. I went and looked at the children, and felt a terrible oppressive sadness, and then I went to Eve's room, and sat on the bed to talk to her. It was a very difficult task I was faced with, but I knew, as MacDown had known, that it had to be me. I felt very bitter about Limbrick who was ultimately responsible for landing me in this position, and my resolve to get out from under hardened even more. I even found myself wondering if Limbrick had chosen me for the job in the first place because he had suspected all along who the negative man was. All in all, it had been too bloody a business for me.

This Large Print Book for the Partially sighted, who cannot read normal print, is published under the auspices of

THE ULVERSCROFT FOUNDATION

THE ULVERSCROFT FOUNDATION

. . . we hope that you have enjoyed this Large Print Book. Please think for a moment about those people who have worse eyesight problems than you . . . and are unable to even read or enjoy Large Print, without great difficulty.

You can help them by sending a donation, large or small to:

**The Ulverscroft Foundation,
1, The Green, Bradgate Road,
Anstey, Leicestershire, LE7 7FU,
England.**
or request a copy of our brochure for more details.

The Foundation will use all your help to assist those people who are handicapped by various sight problems and need special attention.

Thank you very much for your help.

Other DALES Mystery Titles In Large Print